THE DEMONS OF CAMBIAN STREET

CATHERINE CAVENDISH

Copyright © 2012 by Catherine Cavendish
ISBN 978-1-63789-023-3
Macabre Ink is an imprint of Crossroad Press Publishing
All rights reserved. No part of this book may be used or reproduced in any manner whatsoever without written permission except in the case of brief quotations embodied in critical articles and reviews
For information address Crossroad Press at 141 Brayden Dr., Hertford, NC 27944
www.crossroadpress.com

First Crossroad Press Edition - 2023

"You must leave there, you know. There is evil—and I mean tangible evil—in that place. Sarah Asher knew, but not until it was too late to save her. I'm warning you, Stella. You and your husband must get out of that dreadful place as quickly as you can before it all starts again."

"Why? Pattie said much the same thing, but I don't understand."

Rhiannon shrugged. They resumed their walk. "To a nonbeliever, this will sound far-fetched, but I swear every word of what I am going to say is true. You will of course have to make your own mind up."

"Of course. Please go on."

"Did Pattie tell you that Sarah was fifty-five when she fell pregnant for the one and only time in her life?"

"Yes."

"Did she tell you that the baby wasn't Bill's?"

"She told me a story about Sarah saying she had been impregnated by the devil. Surely it was just her hormones or something."

"You can believe that if you want, but I don't think so. Mam always believed, and I believe, that the child wasn't human. That's to say, it looked human but inside, it had no soul and while it was a child, it had no breath."

Dedication

To Colin, without whom...

Acknowledgments

A massive 'thank you' to Crossroad Press for being an amazing publisher

Chapter One

The soft aroma of Badedas bath oil pervaded the air and relaxed her senses as Stella Irwin lay back in the fragrant bubbles. She drifted, the warm water bathing and soothing her, dissolving her fears. She could almost believe there was nothing wrong.

That she had imagined it all.

Then. Without warning. A thunderous crash. Her eyes snapped open. She jerked upright, splashing water onto the floor.

"What the hell was that?" She scrambled to her feet. She was out of the bath and wrapped in her toweling robe in less than a minute.

Panting, she opened the bathroom door a crack. Outside, the hall light was still on, as she had left it. Her gaze took in the empty landing before settling on the old wooden door to her right. Staring at it, her heart beat faster and a corkscrew of panic twisted in her gut.

The bolt was drawn back. Again.

Stella *wasn't* imagining it, but prayed she was wrong.

She sought the only possible explanation, calling her husband's name. "Paul, is that you?"

She listened but heard nothing.

Summoning all the courage she could find, she crept into the hall, lifted the ancient latch, and cracked the closet door open to peek into the darkness. It creaked. She slammed the door shut, bolting it tightly, as she'd done twice before.

Sprinting across the landing, she called again, "Paul? Are you down there?" Silence. Clutching the banister, she made her way down carpeted stairs into the kitchen. She flicked the switch. The fluorescent light shuddered into life, illuminating the newly fitted pine units and gleaming stove. The aroma of boeuf bourguignon emanated from the oven. But Paul wasn't there or in the living room.

Her hands shaking, Stella picked up the phone and pressed number one on the speed dial to reach the main bar of the social club downstairs.

Paul answered on the third ring. "Hi."

"Did you just come up here?" she asked, her voice trembling.

"No, why?"

"I was in the bath and heard a loud crash and the bolt on the closet door on the landing was drawn back even though I knew I had locked it—"

"Stella, you're gabbling. What's happened? Are you OK?"

"Yes. No. Oh, I don't know." She ran her free hand through her still dripping hair.

"Look, Suzannah's here and we're not that busy. She can look after both bars. I'll pop up for a few minutes and investigate that damn cupboard for you once and for all."

Stella replaced the receiver and tried to calm herself. Ever since they had arrived in Priory Saint Michael a couple of months before, their dreams of settling in a peaceful country retreat had started to go awry. Her bout with cancer the previous year had led them to leave Leeds and their hectic city life behind them, and now they lived above the small town's social club where Paul had landed a job as the steward.

But on their first day, Pattie Davies, one of the members, had warned them about the apartment which had lain uninhabited for thirty years. And now Stella wished she'd listened more closely.

Paul's key scraped in the door's lock. He bounded up the stairs. "Good grief, Stella, you're as white as your robe. Come on, let's get you upstairs. You need to lie down."

"I need to get dressed."

"All in good time. Come on."

Still trembling, she followed him upstairs and sat on the bed, her mind racing. What could have caused that crash today—not the first by any means—and, perhaps more disturbingly, how was the bolt being pushed back?

She shoved damp, blond hair out of her eyes and found clothes. Across the landing, she could hear Paul opening the closet door, pushing things around. A few minutes later, dressed in jeans and sweatshirt, she joined him.

Thankfully, Paul had brought a flashlight up from the club. It made a big difference, illuminating dark corners of the unlit walk-in closet she hadn't been able to see clearly before. She scrutinized the cluttered mess of discarded junk: broken bar stools, boxes of old Christmas decorations, and who knew what? Paul had already stacked some boxes on top of each other, clearing a path through to the back and to the left. Only the right side, through another doorway, remained untouched, and that seemed to be filled with an enormous artificial Christmas tree. It was too dark to see beyond it. Too dark to see how far back it went. She shivered. The inky blackness unnerved her, though she tried to tell herself that was her imagination.

Paul was too busy shifting boxes to notice her reaction. He wiped dusty hands on his jeans. "A lot of stuff has been knocked over here, and on these bare boards any of these boxes could have made a loud crash." He flashed the torch to the right. "That was certainly a big tree," he said. "I'll get a couple of the guys to come and help shift it one of these days, along with this other rubbish. My guess is that the vibration from the heavy traffic outside was responsible. After all, we're on the corner of Cambian Street and the High Street, so it's a double whammy. It probably caused something to shake itself loose from wherever it was stacked. Maybe one extra-heavy lorry did the rest. It could quite easily happen, the way they thunder up and down that hill. This whole building shakes sometimes."

"I know. I've felt it." Though calmer, she was still averse to stepping into the cupboard and joining him. It would be like entering another, much older, world. She felt safer with her feet on the newly carpeted landing. Before they had moved in, the whole apartment had been renovated, decorated and modernized, and was now light, bright, comfortable, and clean, even if it did have a little too much beige and cream for her taste. But the building dated from the 1760s and had gone through a number of incarnations. Now only this large closet, tucked under the eaves, bore witness to its past. Its sloping roof, coupled with

Paul's six-foot height, meant he had to stoop uncomfortably low as he moved around.

Although she'd stopped quivering, Stella still couldn't shake off her unease. His explanation for the crashes she had heard since they had moved in made perfect sense, but…

"How did that bolt move? I know I locked it. Just like I did yesterday. And both times it managed to slide across apparently all by itself."

Paul shook his head. "You're right. I can't explain that. But I can get us a new bolt, and I'll do that tomorrow. The little hardware shop across the road will have some." He shifted a broken bar stool out of the way.

Something metallic tinkled. "What's this?" Paul bent to retrieve a silver chain from which hung a circular pendant. "What do you make of that?" He handed it to Stella.

The silver pendant was a mass of interwoven bands. "It looks Celtic to me," she said. "Like a collection of knots, sort of woven together. It's very pretty. I bet someone really missed that when they lost it."

"Wonder how it got up here?"

"No idea. But if you take it down to the club, someone might recognize it. Maybe it belonged to a relative. It's quite distinctive."

"Maybe it belonged to that Sarah Asher they were talking about. The steward's wife who went mad."

"Possibly." Stella looked at her watch. "You'd better get back down there or they'll think you've taken the rest of the day off. I'm going to peel some potatoes."

"Sure you're OK?"

"Yes, I'm fine. I feel better now I've seen this place in the light—well, most of it anyway. It's not so spooky when the corners are lit up." She sounded more confident than she felt, but she didn't want to worry Paul. He had worried enough about her over these past long months.

"Once we get the new bolt on and it stays put, you won't have any nasty shocks."

"True."

Stella backed away to let Paul out. He switched off the flashlight before shutting and bolting the door.

"Where did you get that?" Pattie Davies reached forward and snatched the pendant from Stella's hand.

"Hang on a minute!" Stella tried to take it back.

Pattie clutched it even tighter in her plump fingers. "It's mine," she said, tears welling in her eyes. Around them, a few people murmured. Their comments about Pattie were not complimentary.

Stella glanced up at the clock. 5:10. She looked around the main bar, where a few members chatted over pints of beer. With well-upholstered chairs and polished wooden tables, the club was where the local townsfolk could meet, enjoy a drink, and share the latest news. But Priory Saint Michael was a typical small town in which everyone knew everyone else's business and, right now, Stella needed to afford Pattie some privacy. "Shall we go into the back bar?" she asked gently. "I don't think there's anyone in there yet." With any luck they'd have a few minutes to chat in peace before the noisy after-work crowd arrived for their usual pint on the way home.

Pattie nodded and stood. At a slender five eight, Stella was a good six inches taller than the short, rotund woman who was probably, like her, in her early forties.

Paul carried on serving in the main bar. He'd looked surprised at Pattie's reaction to the pendant, but seemed to have guessed it would be more productive if he left the two women alone to chat.

Stella took a glass of red wine to the back bar and set it in front of Pattie, whose unruly brunette curls fell unheeded into her eyes. She was shredding a tissue, twisting it around her fingers, through which the pendant was intertwined.

Stella sat on the red brocade chair and sipped her gin and tonic, waiting for Pattie to speak.

"When I said this pendant was mine, that wasn't strictly true. It belonged to my mam." Pattie's Welsh accent seemed more pronounced, and she appeared nervous.

"Your mother? How did it get in our upstairs cupboard? Did she lose it here at the club or something?"

Pattie looked up, her cheeks flushed. "I suppose you could say that. Yes, in a way she did really." A faraway look entered her eyes, as though she was remembering something from long ago.

She untangled her fingers from the disintegrated tissue and put it in her bag, found a clean one, and blew her nose. She took a deep breath. "You know about Sarah and Bill Asher who used to live here?"

Stella nodded. "He was the steward thirty years ago and she went mad."

Pattie flinched, and Stella wished she had been a bit more tactful.

"Some people might call it madness, but she was as sane as you and I until…"

Given Pattie's dubious mental reputation, Stella wondered if that was the best of recommendations. She said nothing, and let Pattie continue.

"Anyway, my mam and Sarah Asher grew up together in the thirties. They were neighbors and had known each other since they were babies, so it was only natural they'd be best friends really. Of course, my mam was always different. She had the Gift, you see. My sister has it too, but it seems to have bypassed me altogether."

"The Gift?"

"Second sight. Mam could predict things and sense things around her. She could feel evil as well. She said it had a distinctive taste. Sort of bitter and sour all at the same time." Pattie shuddered. "I always knew when Mam sensed evil. She would look as if someone had forced her to suck a whole lemon. Her mouth would screw up and her eyes would water."

"Sounds bizarre." Stella spoke her thoughts.

Pattie pounced. "You don't believe me, do you? I suppose this is all a big joke to you, isn't it? Batty Welshwoman believes in ghosts and demons! Well, you wait. You need to get out of this place. Six months more in that flat and you'll be begging my sister for her help. Just like Sarah Asher begged my mam all those years ago." Pattie downed her drink and stood.

Stella grabbed her arm. "Pattie, please don't go. I'm so sorry. I don't know what made me say that. What I meant was it's not something I have ever heard of before. It's not something I know anything about."

Pattie hesitated, and Stella fought to maintain what she hoped was a conciliatory, and preferably imploring, expression. She had always liked to keep an open mind about the existence of anything supernatural although if she had to take sides, she would tend toward the skeptical. But this was a two-hundred and fifty year-old building, and Pattie seemed to have an interesting story to tell. Plus, Stella couldn't help but be intrigued to know what had happened to the mysterious Sarah Asher. The very mention of her name had seemed to cause Joe Lloyd, the club's chairman, consternation when Pattie had brought her up before.

Pattie sighed and sat. "All right. I'm sorry I overreacted. It's just that people around here treat me like I'm crazy and I'm not. I can't help it if my mam had the Gift and I can't help what happened to Sarah Asher. However much my mam tried to protect her."

Stella stood. "Why don't I get you another drink and you can tell me what happened. From the beginning."

Pattie hesitated, but the offer of a second glass of wine swayed her. "Thanks. I will. Only could I have the merlot this time? That shiraz is a bit rough."

Stella smiled and went to the bar, and Paul came over, a questioning look in his dark brown eyes. She couldn't talk with him openly so she mouthed, *Later*. He nodded and opened a bottle of merlot. She declined another gin and tonic, her existing one lying mostly untouched on the table.

She returned to Pattie and served the wine. "There you are." She sat and a sharp twinge shot through her stomach, a legacy of her surgery.

"Thanks." Pattie took a sip. When she put down her glass, half its contents had been consumed. "My mam told me that Sarah's husband Bill came from Hereford. He moved here after the war when he got a job at the big agricultural merchant that used to be here. Joe Lloyd's father used to own it. Bill was a good ten years older than Sarah, but apparently he was very handsome. Mam said he looked like a movie star. Like Gregory Peck, she said. I think she was half in love with him herself. Anyway, they got married in the fifties and, in the seventies, Bill Asher lost his job when Lloyd's closed down. They'd both been members here for years so when the post of steward came up, Bill leapt at it. He and Sarah moved into your flat and took over the running of the club. Everything was fine, but cracks in their marriage began to show up." Pattie took another deep swig, becoming visibly agitated.

"It's all right, Pattie, take your time."

Pattie gave a wobbly smile. "Mam said that one day, in 1978 I think it was, Sarah came to her and told her she was pregnant. She was terribly anxious and Mam was incredulous. You see, Sarah was fifty-five years old and Bill was at least sixty-five."

"And was this their first child?" Pattie nodded.

Stella thought for a moment. "Well, it is unusual I suppose, but if she hadn't gone through the menopause—"

Pattie stabbed the table with her forefinger. "But that's the point. She went through the menopause two or three years earlier. She couldn't be pregnant. Sarah was crying and saying how it wasn't Bill's, and Mam was really shocked because Sarah had been a virgin when she married Bill and had never strayed. Neither of them had. Except now Sarah told Mam that she knew for a fact Bill was sleeping with another woman. She didn't know who it was, but it was practically every night. He'd taken to sleeping in the spare room… She'd hear him moaning and she knew what that sound meant."

"Couldn't he have been…you know… masturbating?"

Pattie shook her head. "Sarah said she had heard a woman laughing. When she heard it, she would immediately get out of bed to try to catch her, but Bill was always alone. She did notice a cupboard door was usually open, so she had a bolt put on it. Didn't do much good though."

"Why?"

"Because every night she would bolt it before she went to bed, and every morning, the bolt was drawn back."

Stella's glass slipped through her fingers, its lower edge striking the tabletop. "This cupboard. Was it the closet on the landing?"

"I believe so, yes. Why? Oh no, Stella, don't tell me this is happening to you?"

"No, no, nothing like, well, not like Sarah's experiences. But I have been having problems with the bolt on that door. Paul's going to put a new one on there this evening."

"Let's hope it works."

The door connecting the two bars opened. Joe Lloyd strode in, followed by the club secretary, George Price, and a couple of other men whose names Stella did not yet know. She saw Joe shoot Pattie a disapproving glance. Pattie gulped the rest of her wine and stood.

"Don't go yet, Pattie. Please stay a bit longer or come up to the flat," Stella said.

"No, no I can't do that. I can never come up to that flat. Not after what happened there. And Joe will have me barred from the club if I carry on talking to you about this. He told me so. I'll see you tomorrow perhaps." Pattie shot out of the bar.

Until Pattie had mentioned the cupboard door, Stella had been able to enjoy her tale of the lives of some of Priory Saint Michael's former citizens but as soon as she recounted the detail of the bolt being drawn back every morning, it all became a little too personal.

She took a large swig of her gin and tonic, planning to find out the whole story.

She was still deep in thought when she became aware of Joe's burly figure standing in front of her.

"You mustn't let her get to you with her daft stories. Pattie Davies comes from a line of, shall we say, slightly odd women. Her sister walks around dressed like a hippie from the sixties and her mother was peculiar to say the least. I can remember her coming into the club when Sarah Asher and her husband were still here. I was only in my twenties so it's a good few years ago. She never set foot in here normally. Well, she knew no one would have allowed her to become a member. There's a few too many chapel members here who didn't, and probably still don't, approve of anyone calling herself a witch."

"You mean Pattie's mother?" Stella wished he would get to the point.

He seemed to sense this. "Yes. Her behavior got right up everyone's noses. She made history that night. Only time a non-member has been banned for life!" He laughed.

Stella's impatience was growing. "What did she do?"

"She waltzed in here and Bill was on the bar. She went right up to him and her nose and mouth started to screw right up."

"As if she was sucking a lemon?"

"Yes, that's it! Very good way of describing it. As if she was sucking a lemon. Anyway, she pointed and yelled at him, accusing him of sleeping with an evil spirit. I remember, we all stood there like startled goldfish. Gaping at her as she ranted on and on. Then Sarah appeared, and she was pregnant at the time. She tried to grab hold of Megan, that's Pattie's mother. I suppose Sarah wanted Megan to calm down and leave quietly, but Megan turned on her, with that same pinched-up face, and started accusing *her* of sleeping with the devil. Well that's when we all came to our senses and manhandled her out of there, but I do remember that, as we dragged her out, she pushed something into Sarah's hand. Something on a chain. I never saw what it was but she said something about protection and how she was to wear it and never let it out of her sight."

"What happened to her? Pattie's mother, I mean?"

"She died about ten years ago. In a home."

"Nursing home?"

He nodded and smiled at her as he went to rejoin his friends.

"Stella? You OK?" Paul called. She shook her head and went over to the bar, taking her drink with her. She set it down on one of the many coasters positioned along the highly polished surface.

"I need to talk to Pattie again. As soon as Joe came in, she clammed up, but you should have heard what went on here back in the late seventies when Sarah and Bill Asher were living here."

"You'll have to tell me over dinner. You know, here we were thinking we were coming to a nice, sleepy little backwater and there's all this voodoo and mischief going on."

Stella frowned. "What have you heard? Has someone told you something?"

Paul wiped an imaginary spill with a bar towel, the sort of unnecessary gesture he always made when he was ill at ease about something. "No, of course not, but I could hear something of what Pattie was saying."

Stella decided not to mention the fact that, as he was in the main bar almost all the time, he couldn't have heard Pattie's almost whispered conversation. Granted, the wall between the two bars did not extend through the serving area, but anyone looking after customers in the main bar could not possibly hear a muted conversation in the back. Someone must have been talking to him, maybe saying something which Paul had decided was too much for her to deal with. Well, whatever it was, Stella was determined to find out.

Chapter Two

Stella watched Paul working on the old wooden door. "That bolt had better stay locked tonight," she said, smiling at him.

Smiling back, he replaced the screwdriver in his toolbox. "That bolt is going nowhere. Tonight or any other night. It's solid steel, that is." He tugged at the bolt, which eventually pulled back. "I reckon the other one was worn out."

"It was new when Sarah first found it open every morning."

"My theory is that, either it was the vibration of the traffic wiggling it loose, or else Bill was doing it himself."

"Why, for heaven's sake?"

"Maybe he was sleepwalking...or he was having an affair and his mistress used to hide in the cupboard after closing time. They would have a shag, then she would nip back in there and wait until she was sure Sarah was asleep before leaving."

"Making sure she unset and reset the alarm and didn't wake anyone up. Even though we know that when you first set it, it makes a high-pitched whine that's so piercing you can hear it up here."

"Ah, but they replaced all the alarms in 2005 so maybe the ones in 1978 didn't make that noise. She'd only need to know the code and I guess Bill would have given her that. Unless she was one of the staff, of course. Then she'd have to know it anyway."

"That still doesn't explain the times it's been drawn back when I know I've bolted it." Stella paused and tucked her hair behind her ears.

"OK, Paul, I told you all I know. *You* tell me. What have they told you that I don't know?"

His expression changed from easy to concerned in a flash, and he hesitated before replying. He didn't quite retain eye contact for long enough to reassure her that he was telling her the truth—or, more charitably, *all* the truth.

"A couple of the guys were talking in the bar earlier and they said it was generally believed at the time that Bill Asher was having an affair with Pattie's mother."

Stella's eyes widened. "You have got to be joking! Really?"

Paul nodded. "So they say." He put the flashlight and his toolbox inside the cupboard and bolted the door.

"But what about that episode of her accusing them both of sleeping with devils?"

"They reckon it was staged by Megan—Pattie's mother—to throw Sarah off the scent. It did the job too. The two women never spoke to each other again, as far as anyone knows."

"Has anyone ever said what happened when Sarah had the baby?"

"Not in my hearing." He started to walk down the landing.

"I'd love to know. Think you can find out?"

He stopped, then turned to go downstairs. "I'll see what I can do. Why don't you ask Pattie?"

"I might do that. If I can get her on her own and away from Joe. Whenever he's around she clams up. Apparently Joe said he'd ban her from the Club if she carried on talking to me about it."

"I gather he's chapel. Doesn't hold with witchcraft," Paul called from the stairs over the thump of his shoes on the steps.

Stella took one last glance at the bolt. It was firmly locked. Turning, she followed Paul.

That night, she awoke abruptly from a disturbing dream. The room was pitch dark and, for a moment, she couldn't remember where she was. In the distance she heard girlish laughter and sat up. Perhaps it was wafting in from outside? But the unmoving drapes were drawn tight. Behind them, she knew the small windows were closed. Next to her, the bed was empty. Maybe Paul had gone to the bathroom. She lay for a few minutes, blinking in the dark, wondering whether to switch on the bedside lamp.

She listened. Nothing. Not even a solitary car moving up the hill.

She drifted back to sleep, but her dreams were troubled, and in every single one of them she saw the barmaid, Suzannah. She was smiling, her dark eyes burning as she handed Stella a silver chalice. But when she looked down, it was full of blood. Repelled, she threw it as far away from her as possible, and Suzannah laughed, a terrible echoing sound coming from deep within her.

Stella awoke with a start. Dawn was starting to slip under the curtains. Quiet and still. Next to her, Paul slept on. She tried to get back to sleep but couldn't, disturbed by visions of Suzannah. Stella barely knew the girl, so why? Yet there she was. Laughing at Stella. Mocking her.

What was it about Suzannah?

"How long has Suzannah worked here?" Stella asked as she and Paul sipped their coffee over toast and honey.

"I don't know. Since just before we arrived, I think."

"Local, is she?"

"Yes, I guess so. Why the sudden interest?" "Oh, no reason. Just wondered."

"She's very popular with the members. Always smiling and ready with a bit of banter. Joe was saying the treasurer had told him that the profits are up since she arrived. She does a good job."

Stella longed to ask more but knew Paul would wonder why she was so interested in the girl. After all, there was other bar staff. Why wasn't she showing any curiosity about them? How could she say she'd had a nightmare about Suzannah?

In the large, sunny living room, Stella tied back her newly regrown hair, aware that the short ponytail was much finer than it had been before the chemo.

She sighed. There was no point bemoaning it. She was healthy. Alive. She'd beaten the "Big C." That was all that mattered.

She busied herself with some dusting and vacuuming, repositioning a couple of scarlet rugs on the impractical beige carpet that showed every mark. The club must have got a discount for quantity on the stuff, for it covered almost all of the apartment's floors. Only the tiled kitchen and bathroom had escaped.

Spurred on by her efforts, she experimented with swapping around the chairs and settee of their black leather suite. After further scrutiny, she moved them back again, grateful for the casters.

Feeling a little breathless, she paused by one of the two large windows, looking down at the almost rural scene below. Priory Saint Michael was built on the side of a steep hill, with a narrow, winding river at the bottom, near the church that gave its name to the town. From the living room, Stella could see the ancient building where monks had once walked.

Gravestones in the little cemetery were neatly aligned amid well-maintained green lawns, tranquil and normal. A small country town bathed in autumn sunlight.

She rubbed her stomach, aware of a nagging ache that told her she shouldn't have shifted that furniture around. *That's quite enough for one day, girl.* She turned away from the window and sat at the table to compose her shopping list.

After lunch she went downstairs and, as she was leaving through the bar entrance, she glanced over to see Suzannah pulling a pint of cider and laughing with one of the members.

Looking around, Suzannah met Stella's glance, her gaze penetrating. Stella quickly looked away. That bloody nightmare was making her imagine things.

"See you later, Stella," Suzannah called.

Feeling awkward, Stella pretended she hadn't heard, went outside, and strode the few yards to the end of Cambian Street. She turned left onto the High Street and started to climb up the hill toward the main cluster of small shops. As usual, traffic thundered up and down the busy thoroughfare, the noise almost deafening at this time of day. When two trucks tried to pass each other, she instinctively moved closer to the walls of the houses she passed, certain a set of wheels would mount the sidewalk at any moment.

"Stella, are you all right?" Pattie was coming down the hill on her side of the street.

"Oh, I'm sorry. Hello, yes I'm fine. Just trying to remember what I want from the shops."

"I have that problem all the time. I was thinking of coming down to the club later. Will you be around? There's something I want to talk to you about."

"Yes, I'll be down around nine, I would think."

Pattie hesitated. "How have things been? In the flat I mean?"

"Fine, thanks."

"Nothing untoward at all?"

"Only that damn cupboard I told you about, but Paul's fixed a new bolt on it, so hopefully that will sort the problem out." Stella hesitated. "Pattie, do you know anything about Suzannah, the new barmaid?"

Pattie shook her head. "Don't like her much though. Something about her gives me the creeps. I think she's what they call 'a man's woman.' Not too fond of her own gender because she sees every one of us as competition."

"Yes, that's probably it." "See you later."

Stella spent the rest of the afternoon shopping. She enjoyed buying her meat from the butcher, fruit and vegetables from the greengrocer, and eggs, butter, and milk from the little dairy. Previously, she had always bought everything at the supermarket.

Priory Saint Michael really was in a time warp. The town was neither Welsh nor English, or perhaps it was both, as its boundary had changed a number of times in the past few centuries.

An hour or so later, she made her way down the hill, acknowledging the greetings of some of the club members as she passed them. In a community of only two thousand, everyone pretty much knew everyone else. Even though it meant sacrificing any form of anonymity, Stella found this comforting after the impersonal atmosphere of the big city.

When Stella returned to the club, Suzannah smiled, but was that smile genuine? Or pasted on for the benefit of members? Stella remonstrated with herself. She was letting a stupid dream slip into reality.

She nodded to Suzannah and forced herself to walk steadily through the bar and up to the apartment. Once there, she put away the groceries, grateful for the generous space. The club might not be wealthy, but they certainly hadn't stinted on fitting the apartment. Stella had always wanted a spacious kitchen with plenty of work surfaces and storage space, and now she had it.

Finished, she tucked away her shopping bags on a shelf in the tall cupboard and brewed herself a cup of coffee.

As she sipped, she thought about Suzannah. Had they exchanged more than a handful of words over the weeks? And now, because of one vivid but stupid dream Stella was ascribing all sorts of evil intentions to the poor girl, who wasn't likely to offer anyone a chalice of blood.

Stella drained her coffee mug and washed it, wondering if she was going daft in her middle age. But… Was there something about the girl's eyes? The way she looked at Stella?

She could think of only one way to lay her fantasies to rest: take the initiative and get to know Suzannah. Back rigid with determination, she went down to the bar. There, a few men were leaning up against the bar, chatting. They smiled and greeted her as she came in. Suzannah also smiled.

The TV was on—horse racing from Kempton Park. No one seemed to be paying it much attention except for Sam, the aged afternoon stalwart who sat fiddling with a betting slip and sipping a glass of Guinness.

For the first time, Stella noticed Suzannah's youth, her shiny raven hair and smooth, unblemished skin without a single wrinkle.

"Can I get you anything?" she asked pleasantly.

"Tonic water please," Stella replied, hoisting herself up on a bar stool.

Suzannah opened a small bottle of tonic and poured it into a glass. "Ice and lemon?"

Stella nodded. "There you are."

Stella handed her the money.

"Thanks," she said, before briefly checking it. "Has Paul gone out?" Stella asked.

"No, he's down in the cellar tapping a barrel."

"Oh, right."

Suzannah served another customer while Stella watched unobtrusively. But she sensed that Suzannah was aware she was under scrutiny.

Paul was right. She had a natural way with customers. Especially the men. Some women were natural flirts. Stella sighed. Was she jealous? Suzannah seemed OK. So she knew how to make the most of her looks. Her makeup defined her amazing, almost black eyes, but was understated everywhere else. Her figure-hugging outfits weren't too extreme or revealing. She chatted easily to everyone.

Stella had no reason to be suspicious, but she was. She had no reason to dislike Suzannah, but Stella did.

Paul appeared, wiping his hands on a towel. "Hello love," he said, sounding surprised. "I didn't know you were coming down."

"I'm meeting Pattie at nine."

Edging closer, Paul spoke quietly. "I wish you'd be careful with that one. I've found out a bit more today. She only scraped in as a member and that was because the committee felt sorry for her being on her own and having such a bizarre mother and sister. Joe's serious about banning her. I spoke to him about it today and he's concerned that she's upsetting you."

"Oh, she's all right. A little eccentric maybe, but I don't think there's any harm in her. And I'm not quite the fragile little flower that Joe thinks I am. I'm getting stronger every day and I'll soon be myself again."

"Well, Joe's branded her an out-and-out troublemaker."

"You can tell him from me, I'm a big girl. I can make my own decisions who to be friends with." Irritated, she could imagine how Joe would have delivered his warning about Pattie. *'Tell the little woman to keep away from her. We have to protect our wives. They can easily be led astray if we don't watch it.'*

"Stella, I was only saying that she isn't the most reliable or stable person in the world."

Though she felt quite heated about Paul's warning—to an extent that was disproportionate to his words—she wasn't paying full attention. She was looking at Suzannah who, with no customers to serve, was watching their exchange intently, a smile playing around her lips.

"Stella, did you hear me?"

She switched back to Paul. "Yes, I'm sorry. I'm a little tired. I heard what you said."

"Be careful. That's all. Nothing heavy." Paul's glance shifted.

Pattie arrived. "Hello!"

Stella turned to her. "Hi, Pattie. Merlot?"

"That would be lovely."

"I'll have some gin in my tonic, Paul." Stella slid off the bar stool and found a nearby table, Pattie following. Paul brought their drinks.

"You were going to tell me more about this place," Stella said. "And about that poor woman, Sarah Asher."

Pattie sipped her wine and looked quickly around, no doubt making sure Joe wasn't near. She said, "You have to remember that I was only a small child at the time this was all going on, but my mam told me that Sarah came to her one day, when she was pregnant, and begged her to help her get rid of it. She said it was the child of the devil and that it would kill her. Mam thought it was her hormones going mad with the pregnancy, but Sarah was adamant that one evening she had woken up to find what she thought was a strange man in her bed. He had held his hand over her mouth to stop her screaming. She said a woman had held her legs so that she couldn't kick out. The man got on top of her and it was he who got her pregnant. When she saw his face, she knew he was a demon."

Stella stared at her. "Did your mother believe her?"

Pattie shrugged. "Mam was never one to doubt that there were evil forces at work in the world and she knew of the legends surrounding this place."

"Legends?"

"Oh yes. For centuries, people have talked about witches and demons around Cambian Street. You ask the vicar."

"And Sarah Asher didn't know the man or the woman? Where was her husband when this was going on?"

"I don't know that, but I do know Sarah told my mam that Bill Asher admitted that a beautiful young woman would visit him at night and he would have sex with her. He said he would wake up and find himself in the spare bedroom with no idea how he got there and a recurring dream about going into the cupboard on your landing and finding himself in another room he didn't recognize."

"As if the cupboard was some sort of entrance?" "That's what Mam thought. He could describe this room in minute detail, down to the purple drapes hanging on the walls. He said there were no windows, just these drapes and an altar with black candles. Oh, and he said there was always a strong smell of perfume. One of the expensive ones, but he didn't know which."

"It's an incredible story. Obviously your mother didn't help her to get rid of the baby."

"She did try, but not by any means other than an exorcism. Mam performed a witches' spell to cast out the demon within her, but it clearly didn't work because the baby was born and Sarah died. Bill was never the same after that."

Pattie seemed about to say more, but Joe came in and glared at her. She drained her glass with a shaking hand. "Thank you for the drink. I think I'd better go."

Stella wished Joe hadn't picked that moment to appear but sensed she couldn't persuade Pattie to stay. Pattie had also made it plain she wouldn't feel comfortable going up to the flat. Still, they could always resume their chat another day.

"I'll see you soon."

Pattie leaned toward her. "Watch out for that Suzannah," she whispered. "She's got her eye on your husband."

"Don't be daft. He's at least twenty years older than her."

"Nevertheless…"

The problem was, Stella realized, she had much the same thought herself.

That night, she woke again to a dark room whose only light came from the streetlamp outside, and no Paul. Stella rubbed her eyes, the sound of girlish laughter drifting in to her. She sat up, caught a movement out of the corner of her eye and saw something scurry across the floor. She screamed, and light flooded the room.

"Whatever's the matter?" Paul was standing at the door, naked. In an instant he was holding her to him, cuddling her shaking body. "You've had a nightmare. That's all it is."

"I saw something. I think we've got rats. Bloody big ones at that."

"It was probably a trick of the light. Look, if it makes you feel any better, I'll check under the bed.

Hang on." He knelt and peered under. "There's nothing here. Which way did you see it go?"

"Towards the window—or maybe—oh, I don't know! It all happened so fast. And it was an odd shape. Sort of hunched. Oh God, I'm not making any sense, am I?"

Paul emerged from under the bed and stood. "I think you'd woken up from a bad dream, a car went past outside, and its headlights made a shadowy pattern through the curtains. Your brain did the rest. Not surprising after an evening in Pattie's company. What did you talk about? Ghosts and ghouls and things that go bump in the night?"

Despite her fright, Stella smiled and said nothing, hoping he was right. Paul switched off the light and got back into bed as Stella sank into the pillow. He leaned over and kissed her. "Snuggle up to me and let's go back to sleep."

"That sounds like a good idea," she said, turning over and putting her arm around him. Almost immediately she started to drift off, an aroma of Chanel Number Five in her nostrils.

As she approached the closed cellar door, Stella recognized Suzannah's voice on the other side. At one thirty in the afternoon, no staff was in either bar though it was Suzannah's shift. So what was she doing in the cellar, having a laugh with someone? And who was she with anyway?

She opened the door silently.

Suzannah's blouse was unbuttoned enough to expose an impressive cleavage encased in a low-cut black bra.

And Paul was reaching out, about to caress one of her breasts.

Suzannah spotted Stella and pushed his hand away.

"What the hell's going on here?" Stella clenched her fists, fighting to keep them by her sides. Anger and dismay fought for control within her as she glared at Paul.

He tore his eyes away from Suzannah's breasts as she buttoned her blouse. "I was changing a barrel," he said hurriedly, his face betraying him.

"And I bet you were showing Suzannah how to do it, weren't you? It all got a bit hot down here so she undid her blouse to cool off and you were helping to wipe the sweat off her tits!"

"No. I—"

"Oh, spare me your excuses and lies, Paul. I want her out of here. Now! She's fired." Stella turned and, with as much dignity as she could gather, left the room.

As the door closed behind her, she heard Suzannah giggle.

Stella poured herself two shots of Scotch, added a chunk of ice, and downed it, immediately refilling her glass. She took a table near the bar and struggled with herself until Paul and Suzannah returned.

To her amazement, they worked the bar as though nothing had happened. Members were coming in to watch the horse racing on TV or for an afternoon drink, and they were served swiftly and smoothly.

Had she imagined what she'd seen? Hadn't her husband groped that girl's tits? Hadn't she told him to fire her? What was going on here? Stella finished her drink and went to the bar.

"Another?" Suzannah asked brightly.

Stella summoned up equilibrium from nowhere and kept her voice low, so as not to attract an audience. "I wish to speak to my husband."

Suzannah shrugged and served another customer. Paul came over. At least he had the grace to look shamefaced.

"What's going on?" she snarled.

One or two of the members were starting to take an interest in their conversation.

"Not here, Stella, please. Later."

"No. Now. Upstairs." She stalked toward their apartment's door, where she turned to check he was following her.

Paul hesitated, exchanging glances with Suzannah, whose black ponytail seemed even more glossy and bouncy today. Stella longed to wipe that bloody smirk off Suzannah's smug little face.

He followed Stella upstairs, but she kept her silence until they were in the living room. "What the hell do you think you were playing at down in that cellar? And how long has this been going on anyway? Are you sleeping with the little tart?"

Paul tried to put his hands on Stella's shoulders, but she shrugged him off and backed away.

"Look, Stell, I know you won't believe me, but I swear I have never touched the girl before today. I don't even know why I did! It was like I said. I went down to change a barrel. Suzannah followed me and made some remark about me having a nice arse. I was bending down at the time. I stood up to say thank you and instead, I told her she has a nice rack. Honestly Stella, I have no idea why I said that or what came over me. She unbuttoned her blouse and asked me if I would like to feel them. That's when you walked in. I swear to you, nothing else happened and nothing else has ever happened. I've never even thought about her like that. I mean, she's a very pretty girl, but she must be half my age and I'm no cradle snatcher. I love you, Stella. I am so sorry."

Her eyes never left his face as he gave her the line used by so many unfaithful husbands caught philandering, but she had known Paul a very long time. They had been married fifteen years. At forty- five he could still pass for a man ten years younger. True, the dark brown hair was tinged with gray, but that did nothing to diminish his good looks. If he wanted to, he could find plenty of women to fool around with, but he had never been like that. In all their years together, she had never had any cause to doubt him. Through the last eighteen months, he'd been by her side through an awful battle with cancer, never wavering in his support.

His reaction persuaded her that this time, *this* husband was telling the truth.

After a lengthy pause, during which Paul seemed to be holding his breath, she trusted herself to speak.

"Your face will turn purple if you hold your breath any longer," Stella said quietly. "I'll forgive you. This time. But she has to go. This has to be her last shift, and I never want to see her again in this club. Preferably not in Priory Saint Michael. Is that understood?"

Paul nodded. "I can't do anything about where she lives, but I'm pretty sure I can fire her and I will. Right now. I'm afraid it's up to the committee whether or not she is banned from the club, although I will recommend it to them, and I'll tell her I would prefer not to see her in here again. That's really all I can do. Stella, I am so, so sorry about this. The last thing I ever want to do is hurt you."

He held his arms open, and she went to him, nestling against his chest and hearing his heart beating too quickly. She could tell this had really shaken him. And at least that little trollop was getting her comeuppance!

Paul went back down to the bar, and Stella made herself a cheese sandwich, figuring the bread would soak up four shots of whisky. Weary, she lay on the settee and remembered Pattie's warning. Maybe Paul really was innocent this time, but she would have to watch Suzannah. The girl was trouble. Of that she was certain.

A couple of hours later, Stella climbed the stairs and went into the bedroom. She opened one of the wardrobes and took out her long toweling bathrobe. She stripped, put it on, and threw her sweater and underwear into the wicker laundry basket by the dressing table. After neatly folding her jeans, Stella tucked them away on one of the many wardrobe shelves. Passing the cupboard on the landing, she glanced at the bolt and was gratified to see it firmly locked. Shutting the bathroom door, she turned on the shower, losing herself in its steamy and aromatic caresses.

Ten minutes later, she got out and toweled herself dry. The shock of seeing Paul with Suzannah seemed to have dissolved in the hot water.

She opened the bathroom door and stood stock still, staring at the drawn bolt on the cupboard door.

She screamed once. Twice. More. Gut-wrenching, agonized screams. She lurched into the bedroom. Paul dashed in as she shivered and trembled, hunched on the bed, her wet, disheveled hair dripping into her eyes and down her neck.

"Whatever is it? I could hear you downstairs." He sat beside her, drawing her close to him.

"What's happening to me, Paul? How can that bolt be drawn back? It was locked when I went into the bathroom."

"Hang on here for a second, I'll go and check."

He was back within seconds. "It must have been a trick of the light, Stell. The door's bolted. Come and see for yourself."

He took her hand, and she allowed him to lead her to the door. She stared at the bolt in disbelief. Just as Paul had said. Locked.

"I know what I saw." Why wouldn't he believe her?

"Well, I didn't touch it. I'm sorry, Stell, but you must have been mistaken. It's easy to misinterpret things, isn't it?"

If that was a veiled reference to earlier, Stella didn't appreciate it. She glared at him and shook off his hand. "I'm going to get dressed."

Later that evening, down in the club, Stella sipped a gin and tonic at the bar as she listened to a group of regulars, all men of varying ages from twenty-something upward, chatting animatedly about Suzannah. She'd left, and Paul was serving in the back bar.

"No idea where she used to work, have you, Les?" George asked.

Les, a local farmer, shook his head. "As far as I know, she turned up here one day looking for work." He nodded over at Stella. "Just before you two came here. Makes a lovely change having a pretty face behind that bar. Saves us from having to look at Mike's ugly mug all day!"

"Watch it," said Mike, the senior barman. Grinning, he handed Les a pint of Guinness.

"Legs right up to her armpits, that one, and a lovely pair of tits. Could have lost myself in those tits."

"Now, Les, there's a lady present." Mike nodded over at Stella.

"Oh, don't mind me," she said. "I'm curious to know more about her. Where does she live?"

"In the next village, I think. Rokesby Green. Someone said she lived in a mobile home but I wouldn't know. She looks a little gypsyish though, don't you think? Those dark eyes and all that black hair."

"Don't you start again, Les. She'd eat you up for breakfast anyway!"

The others laughed, and Les smiled good- naturedly. He was in his sixties and his face bore the hallmarks of a lifetime spent outside in all weathers. "You're probably right," he said. "Mind you, if I was married to anyone she set her cap at, I'd take care." He looked straight at Stella. "I'd take a great deal of care."

Stella nodded and sipped her drink. "Anyway, she doesn't work here anymore, so we won't be seeing her around here."

"What do you mean she doesn't work here? She was here earlier," Mike said. "And no one said anything to me about her leaving."

"Paul fired her. Her work wasn't up to scratch."

"Eh?" Mike exchanged glances with the men and fingered his graying beard. "He can't do that. I mean, it's not his place to fire anyone. The committee has to make that decision and the secretary does the hiring and firing. Officially anyway. Paul can recommend a dismissal of course, but that's as far as he can go."

Stella looked around the sea of bemused faces, most of which wore raised eyebrows. "I expect that's what he's done. But she will be leaving. Soon."

"What do you think they meant, Paul?" Stella asked him later in the evening in their living room. "You told her she was going, didn't you?"

Paul squirmed. "Not exactly." "What do you mean, 'not exactly'?"

"I did what I am allowed to do in these circumstances. I told her that I didn't see how we could carry on working together after what had happened earlier today and that I felt she should do the decent thing and leave."

"And what did she say?"

"She said she'd let the committee decide."

"Oh fine! And meanwhile, she's allowed to carry on working here. How do you think that makes me feel, Paul?"

"Not great, I should imagine."

"That's an understatement."

"Look, I'm sorry. I thought I had the power to fire her, but it's a good job Joe was in and I had the sense to check with him first or all hell could have broken loose. She could have sued me for wrongful dismissal and all sorts of stuff."

"Don't you think all hell has broken out anyway? Or at least it's going to if I see that woman in the bar again."

"Perhaps you'd better not come down to the bar until it's sorted out," he said quietly.

"*What?* Why should I do that when I've done nothing wrong?"

"Because it will only upset you and you're supposed to be getting yourself strong again."

"So, I have to give up my social life for a little tart who can't keep her hands off my husband. Great!"

"Oh come on, Stella, it wasn't that big a deal. So she flashed her tits at me? And very nice they were too. It was quite flattering for a forty-something male to be flashed by a gorgeous young girl with a firm body and—"

She stood, and he stopped.

"I have scars," she said. "My hair fell out because of the chemo, and it hasn't been the same since. I'm forty-three. I know all that. *You* need to know it's her or me. Make a choice." She turned to leave the living room. "And thanks, Paul. It's good to find out where I stand."

"Stella, please, I'm sorry, I didn't mean it the way it came out. Stella!"

But she was in no mood to listen.

Chapter Three

Stella awoke a little after two a.m. She was alone in bed and, as before, she heard a girl laughing. Half asleep, she pushed back the duvet and got out of bed without switching on the light. The bedroom door was partially open, and she went out onto the landing. The sound of laughter was a little louder. As if in a dream, she shuffled toward the bathroom, hearing voices too indistinct to translate into words. She stopped at the closed spare bedroom door and reached for the knob when she heard the laughter again.

She turned. The laughter seemed to be coming from behind the closed cupboard door. She could barely see anything and wished she had put on the landing light as there was no switch at this end. The bathroom light would help, so she reached around the door for the light pull and tugged it. The extractor fan whirred into life, and the light illuminated the landing sufficiently for her to see that the bolt was again drawn back. Still more asleep than awake, she lifted the latch and tentatively opened the door.

She heard scurrying. Two gleaming red eyes stared at her and she screamed, half-falling into Paul's arms as he appeared on the landing behind her.

"Good grief, Stella, you gave me such a fright." She let him lead her back to bed. "I went downstairs to get a glass of water and when I came up I saw you opening the cupboard."

"I saw red eyes. They looked at me." She heard her own words. How crazy they sounded. "Oh, God, Paul, I don't know what's happening. I feel like I'm going mad. What was that I saw?"

"I think you'd better see a doctor. These nightmares are getting worse."

"I wasn't asleep. It was real."

"Stella, the only thing in that cupboard is junk." "I was awake!"

"You've been listening to Pattie."

"You have to believe me. There's something in there. I saw it." Hot tears welled up and flooded her eyes.

"Come on, love, lie down." Paul gently steered her back and tucked her under the duvet before joining her.

Despite her fears, exhaustion finally overwhelmed her and she turned to him, drifting off as she curled around him. She smelled a familiar scent...again. "Paul?" she asked, as she fell asleep. "Why are you wearing Chanel Number Five?"

"Have you heard about Pattie Davies?"

Stella turned from the notice board and saw the perturbed club secretary, shaking his dripping umbrella in the doorway.

"Heard what?" she asked.

"She's dead. Killed by a speeding motorist yesterday night."

"What?"

"Yes, terrible it is. Around midnight it was. She must have been a bit distracted. Or maybe she'd had too much to drink, because she didn't use the crossing at the bottom of the hill. She crossed just before it and this motorist caught her. Never stopped neither."

Queasy, Stella sat on a bench. "She was killed by a hit and run driver? Do the police have any idea who did it?"

"Not yet. I'm surprised I'm the one to tell you. It's all over the town this morning. I felt sure someone would have been in or rung you. Apparently, after it happened, you couldn't move for police and the ambulance. Blocked the road off for an hour or more."

Pattie, *dead?* Stella couldn't believe it. "It's still early, and Paul's been dealing with a delivery. I've not been up long. Didn't have a very good night's sleep." She was speaking like an automaton while she tried to sort out her thoughts.

"It's been on the local radio this morning."

"Never listen to the radio in the mornings these days." The buzzing in her head told her she was in danger of fainting. She didn't want George to see her make a total fool of herself, so she made her excuses and escaped. Her hands were clammy and trembling as she unlocked the door to the flat.

The buzzing louder, she had a sensation of moving in slow motion, struggling to the top stair. Stella sank down on it, her head between her legs and stayed there for ten minutes or maybe more, glad of the peace and quiet. She concentrated on remaining conscious and keeping her breathing steady while she thought things through.

Poor Pattie. Stella knew so little about her, but she seemed to have led a sad, troubled, and unfulfilled life. She had died as she had lived—alone—and, unless the hippie sister turned up, few would mourn her.

She leaned back against the banister and waited for the nausea and lightheadedness to pass. At least the buzzing had stopped and she didn't feel faint anymore.

As the minutes ticked by, she began to feel a little better until, finally, she trusted herself to try to stand.

Once on her feet, she decided to go back downstairs.

The bar was busy. One topic was on everyone's lips: Pattie Davies' death.

"They should lock that driver up and throw away the key."

"She wasn't a bad old girl."

"Less of the old. She was younger than me." "Terrible way to go. Who could run someone over and leave them there?"

"Maybe they didn't. Maybe they stopped, got out of the car, saw she was dead, and panicked. Not a lot of people around at that time of night during the week. Most folk are asleep."

"What about the houses that look out onto that part of the road?" Stella asked Joe. "Didn't anyone there get woken up and come to investigate? There must have been a screeching of brakes."

"You know, that's the funny thing," he replied. "I heard the police have questioned anyone within possible earshot and no one reported hearing any brakes squealing. One chap said he couldn't sleep and was in his kitchen making a mug of hot milk. He was only yards away from where it happened at the time. Of course, his curtains were drawn and he does have double glazing, but he said he couldn't understand why he didn't hear anything. It's as if whoever hit her kept on going. Never even attempted to stop."

A man Stella didn't know piped up from the opposite end of the bar. "If that was old Cecil Jones, it's more likely he didn't have his hearing aid in. Deaf as a post without it, he is!" A chorus of laughter accompanied this, but Stella couldn't find even a trace of a smile.

"The thing is," she said, later that evening when she and Paul were relaxing in front of the TV, "I heard from George later that Pattie's body showed that the car had run right over her and, when I went down to the supermarket earlier, I looked for the tire marks. There weren't any. Surely if you hit someone, you automatically slam on the brakes, the tires lock, you screech to a halt, and you leave tread marks all over the road."

"Ah, but with some of these modern braking systems, they're so efficient they brake quickly but you don't swerve, and I guess you wouldn't leave the sort of marks you're thinking of."

"But it didn't stop smoothly, did it? It ran right over her."

"Well, that would slow it down, wouldn't it? It would have been like running over a cushion."

"Paul, this isn't funny. A woman has been killed by a hit and run driver and all you can do is make inane jokes about her weight!"

"Oh come on, Stella, you hardly knew her. What are you getting so upset about?"

"I'm not getting upset. It's a bit of a shock to find that someone you were only speaking to a couple of days ago is dead." Tears filled her eyes.

Paul knelt in front of her and took her hands in his. "Come here, love." He drew her to him.

She leaned against his shoulder. "I'm going to the funeral," she said in a tone she knew Paul would recognize as final.

He drew back. "You could find yourself the only guest. She wasn't exactly noted for her wide circle of friends and apart from her dippy-sounding sister, no one seems to know of any relatives either."

"All the more reason I should go. My mind's made up. First thing tomorrow, I'm going to find out where her sister lives and I'm going to see her. I'll offer to help make the arrangements if she needs that too."

Paul looked pained, but said nothing.

Stella immediately knew that the woman in the floor length, black velvet dress with coppery hair hanging to her waist and an ankh around her neck was Pattie's sister. She was alone, clearly lost in her own thoughts, as she sat on a bench overlooking the gently flowing river.

Stella approached her, and the woman turned around, shielding her eyes from the autumn sun with her hand.

"You must be Rhiannon. I'm Stella. My husband is the new steward at the Priory Club."

"Yes, you would be. Pattie told me the new people had come."

"I'm so sorry to hear about your sister. We were only chatting earlier this week. She was telling me all about the club in the old days. Sarah and Bill Asher..."

Rhiannon's eyes flashed. "You would do well to keep in mind what my sister said about those two."

"What do you mean? I'm sorry, I didn't mean to make you angry. Especially not at such a sad time."

Rhiannon took a deep, slightly ragged breath. "No, I'm sorry. I shouldn't have jumped at you like that. It's... Look, why don't we walk for a bit along the river. I'm atrophying sitting here."

Stella nodded and Rhiannon stood. An icy breeze chilled Stella's cheeks and blew dry leaves across their path as they strolled beside the river. She thrust her cold hands deep into the pockets of her warm winter coat, wishing she had remembered gloves.

"Sarah Asher was the victim in that sad affair." Rhiannon said. "Of course you may not believe in it. Many don't and around here if you mention the word 'witch,' all the churchgoers throw up their hands in horror and run away, afraid they may hear something that causes them to question their beliefs. I've always thought it strange myself. I mean, I would imagine I know the Bible at least as well as most of them. It's brimful of demons and devils, and yet whenever our mam used to point the finger, she was ridiculed and ostracized. At least in my case, they leave me alone and let me get on with it."

"So you *are* a witch?"

She nodded. "I'm what a lot of people call a white witch. Yes, I cast spells and recite incantations. I celebrate the great Wiccan festivals and have even been known to dance naked around a fire. But I don't cackle over a cauldron of steaming eyes of toad and wing of bat and have never been known to curse anyone's cattle, sheep, or errant son. So you can toss all those preconceived ideas right out of your head." Rhiannon gave a light laugh.

Stella felt relieved. She had thought her new acquaintance was growing a little agitated. "I don't really have any preconceived ideas to toss away. As I said to Pattie, witchcraft and demons are new territories for me, although there have been some odd things going on in the flat."

Rhiannon stopped. "You must leave there, you know. There is evil—and I mean tangible evil—in that place. Sarah Asher knew, but not until it was too late to save her. I'm warning you. You and your husband must get out of that dreadful place as quickly as you can before it all starts again."

"Why? Pattie said much the same thing, but I don't understand."

Rhiannon shrugged. They resumed their walk. "To a nonbeliever, this will sound far-fetched, but I swear every word of what I am going to say is true. You will of course have to make your own mind up."

"Of course. Please go on."

"Did Pattie tell you that Sarah was fifty-five when she fell pregnant for the one and only time in her life?"

"Yes."

"Did she tell you that the baby wasn't Bill's?"

"She told me a story about Sarah saying she had been impregnated by the devil. Surely it was just her hormones or something."

"You can believe that if you want, but I don't think so. Mam always believed, and I believe, that the child wasn't human. That's to say, it *looked* human but inside, it had no soul and while it was a child, it had no breath."

Stella shook her head. "I'm sorry, Rhiannon, you'll have to take small steps with me. I don't understand any of that."

"Have you ever heard of a creature called an incubus? Or a succubus?"

Stella searched her brain. The two words were vaguely familiar. "I think I may have read a horror novel, or seen a film with something like that in it."

"Forget Hollywood. These creatures are real. They're demons. They may look like us during the day, but at night they change. Some of them are pretty versatile shape-shifters and can alter their appearance to whatever they choose at will, but they can't reproduce by themselves. To do that, they need human hosts. The succubus is a female demon who mates with the human male and collects his sperm, which she passes onto the male demon, the incubus. He then transmits it to a human female, fertilizes her egg, and a child is produced that is neither human nor demon. It is a half-breed of both and is known as a cambion. Sarah's child was just such a creature."

Stella's mind tumbled with thoughts like a waterfall. This couldn't be real. She couldn't believe she was walking calmly along a riverbank listening to a woman who called herself a witch, proclaiming that the child of one of her neighbors was a demon!

She tried to make some sense of it. "So if this child really was alive, what happened to it? And what happened to Bill?"

"You know that Sarah died in childbirth."

Stella nodded. "Pattie told me."

"Well, as with so many of these births, the baby was premature, but fully formed. The midwife was called as there wasn't time to get her to the hospital. The labor was all over in a couple of hours, but there were complications and Sarah contracted septicemia. They fought hard for her at the hospital, but she died three days later, screaming and incoherent. All anyone could tell was that she was praying for forgiveness. Bill lost it completely. He wouldn't go back to the club. He said a devil was out to get him, and he ended up in a mental hospital. Died there two years later. The baby was apparently born dead. As I said, a cambion has no breath. But the midwife took the baby, saying she would take it to the hospital in her car. No one ever saw her again. No one had ever seen her before either. She had said she was the relief midwife because the usual woman was on holiday. That wasn't true, any more than the baby being dead was true. The real midwife was at home, tucked up in bed sound asleep. Whoever that other woman was, she knew the baby would be born that night. She intercepted the call before the phone could wake up the real midwife."

They stopped, and Stella struggled to keep a sense of reality. She picked up a small stone and threw it far into the river, hearing it plop into the water. The ripples spread increasing circles, predictable and therefore calming. Stella needed that.

"So they never heard any more about what happened to the baby? Or where it might be now?"

Rhiannon shook her head and turned her hazel gaze to meet Stella's. "No, but she would be in her early thirties. She would be very beautiful, very cunning, and very manipulative, especially in regard to men. Cambions are. They are capable of causing even the best of men to commit unspeakable acts."

"Are they always female?"

"No. In legend, we are told that Merlin was a cambion and Shakespeare's Caliban in 'The Tempest' was one as well."

Stella tried to take it all in. "So what do you think happened to the demons?"

"Can't you guess?"

Stella met the steady hazel eyes. Something inside her chest jerked in shock. "Oh my God, you mean you think they're still in the flat. Don't you?"

Rhiannon nodded. "I'm very much afraid so. Now do you see why you have to get out of there?"

"Stella? It's Rhiannon. I thought I'd let you know, they've released Pattie's body and the funeral is next Tuesday. Will you come?"

"Of course. Do you want us to lay on a buffet for guests here at the club?"

"That's very kind of you, but no. I don't think many will want to come and I'd rather keep it quiet. Pattie would have preferred it if only those who cared about her attended. That leaves you and me and possibly a couple of stray aunts from Llangollen. Is that OK?"

"Of course. You must do what feels right. If I don't see you before, I'll see you there. Is it at the priory?"

"Oh sorry, I didn't tell you. No, it's not. Neither Pattie nor I are Christians, so it would seem a bit hypocritical, wouldn't it? As High Priestess, I'll be conducting a Wiccan funeral. Art, a friend of mine from Glastonbury, is coming up to take part as the High Priest. It's actually a very beautiful ceremony. If you've never been to one before, I'm sure you'll like it. Art's daughter will take the part of the Maiden. That's another important role in the ritual. The coven will assist with the other roles and there'll be wine and cakes afterward. After that, we'll go up to the crematorium. It's all starting at ten-thirty at my house."

"What should I wear?"

"Anything you like. We have our ceremonial robes of course, but you and the two aunts can dress as you would normally for a funeral."

When she had finished the call, Stella replaced the receiver, smiling at herself. Witchcraft? Demons? And all part of her daily diet? She was going crazy. It was the only possible explanation.

To reach Rhiannon's home, Stella walked down to the bottom of the hill, crossed the street, and made her way along a short, narrow lane of small, terraced cottages. Rhiannon's was easy to find. It was the only one with a purple front door and wind chimes, clinking gently in the light breeze.

She had barely rung the bell when the door opened and Rhiannon, dressed in ceremonial robes of green and gold, greeted her with a kiss on both cheeks. "Come in and meet everyone."

Stella smiled and stepped into Rhiannon's living room.

The cottage was probably older than the club, with low, timbered ceilings. The room Stella entered was small and packed with twelve people, all standing, chattering as though the occasion was a cocktail party rather than a wake. They greeted Stella with smiles and handshakes. Incense gave off a heady scent of cedar while logs crackled in the grate. The warm, cozy room was a sharp contrast to the chilly, late autumn day.

Rhiannon handed Stella a small glass of a golden, sticky liquid. "Mead," she answered Stella's unasked question. "It's traditional. You may find this a little shocking. But we're happy that Pattie's soul is passing into the paradise we call Summerlands. We don't mourn her death to this life, but celebrate her birth in her new one."

"I think that's a lovely way of looking at it," Stella said and took her first ever sip of mead. It was like drinking honey. Far too sweet for her taste, but it certainly had a kick as it warmed its way down into her stomach, leaving behind a pleasant, mellow glow. Just sufficient for her to lay aside her reticence and mingle with the members of the coven who were dressed in an array of ceremonial robes, Goth black velvet, and hippie chic.

The Wiccan funeral was a surprisingly moving affair. In the end, the two aunts from Llangollen had felt too frail to make it. "They're in their eighties and don't really approve of all this," Rhiannon explained. "They're chapel, you see. My mam was from the other side of the family."

"Must make it awkward."

"Families. Who'd have them?" Rhiannon smiled. Once the coven and Stella were assembled,

Rhiannon and her friend, the High Priest, stood with their backs to the altar and addressed them.

Rhiannon's voice was pure and unwavering. "We meet today to mark the passing of our beloved sister, Pattie, for whom this incarnation is ended." On the altar was a small earthenware bowl with a silver cord tied around it by Art's daughter in her role as the Maiden.

A lengthy invocation followed, and Stella stepped back so as not to interfere with a ritualistic spiral dance performed by the entire coven. The High Priest spoke, invoking the Earth Mother. "We commend to thee, Pattie, our sister. Take her, guard her, guide her, admit her to the peace of Summerlands." He took a cloth, wrapped the bowl, and smashed it with a hammer.

A collective gasp went up around the coven.

Stella felt as if she was being pulled toward the altar and had to resist the temptation to move closer.

The ritual continued with invocations to the Lords of the Watchtowers of the West and East and a further invocation to the Earth Mother. Roles had been assigned to coven members, including one who was the Goddess and was duly adorned with jewelry and a veil, only to have them stripped off her, so that she stood before them in a plain, full-length shift. A red cord was wound around her in ceremonial fashion, her wrists bound behind her waist.

A coven member, as Lord of the Underworld, performed further ceremonies with her until finally, the ritual completed, the High Priest took a chalice of wine. "Let us now, as the Goddess hath taught us, share the love-feast of the wine and cakes. And with this Communion we lovingly place our sister in the hands of the Goddess."

The coven uttered a collective, "So mote it be," and the consuming of wine and cakes commenced.

"So what did you think?" Rhiannon, still in her robes, handed Stella a delicious-looking strawberry shortcake.

"Very moving. But it seems odd that she wasn't here."

Rhiannon frowned. "She was. Oh, I see, you mean the coffin wasn't here? No, that is still with the undertaker. We're going up to the crematorium this afternoon. Would you like to come?"

Stella nodded.

"You see, we don't need her physical body to be here in order to commit her spirit to the Earth Mother. Pattie's spirit was with us and that is what she is now."

Stella was moved by the unquestioning belief and simplicity of it all. She wished she had a faith to draw on that was as powerful as Rhiannon's.

Stella picked up her car from the club and drove Rhiannon to the crematorium which, by contrast, seemed cold and impersonal. Most of the coven had chosen to attend, in order to support their High Priestess, but still there were so few. Not even two rows of the small chapel were filled. Afterward, Stella took Rhiannon home.

"Have you thought any more about what I said the other day?" Rhiannon asked.

"I haven't spoken to Paul about it yet." Rhiannon frowned.

"Things have been a bit difficult and I'm quite sure he already thinks I'm flaky."

She nodded, looking unhappy, and asked, "What do you know about that barmaid, Suzannah?"

Stella was taken aback at the unexpected question. Why should Rhiannon ask about *her?* She kept her voice steady. "Not much. Only that she lives in Rokesby Green and appeared one day looking for a job."

"Find out what you can about her. I'll do the same. There's something about her that concerns me."

Stella stopped the car outside Rhiannon's cottage. "You know something don't you?"

Rhiannon inhaled. "I'm not sure. It's that place. That bloody flat you're living in. The club. The whole street actually."

Stella put her hand on her friend's velvet-clad arm. "You must tell me."

Rhiannon rubbed her forehead. "The name of the street. Cambian Street. Do you know where it comes from?"

"Surely it's a misspelling of Cambrian. After all, we're right on the Welsh border. I think Priory Saint Michael was actually in Wales until the boundary changes in the seventies."

Rhiannon shook her head. "Oh, it's a misspelling all right. A misspelling of cambi*on*. There are reports of hauntings and demonic activity going way back to the thirteenth century. Exorcisms were carried out regularly up and down that street. Especially in the houses which now make up the club. There were reported cases of demonic possession, casting out of devils, succubi, incubi, and devil children. Cambions. It sort of stuck."

"Good grief!"

"I'm sorry, Stella, but there's more. I have a suspicion about Suzannah. I have seen her around the town and every time she sees me, she avoids my eye and dashes off somewhere. She's hiding something, and I have a horrible taste in my mouth every time I see her. I don't know for sure, but I think she may be a cambion. I've seen one before, and she was beautiful too. Too beautiful."

A thought flashed into Stella's mind. "You don't think she could be Sarah Asher's daughter, do you?"

Rhiannon thought about this for a moment. "That would put her in her early thirties. She only looks about twenty, but it *is* possible. They can perpetuate their beauty and youthfulness so, maybe, yes. But even if she isn't, she *is* dangerous. Remember, I told you that incubi and succubi can look just like us in daylight. So can cambions." She grabbed Stella's hand. "You and Paul have got to leave there because if I'm right, nothing good will come of this. Someone, maybe even you, is in mortal danger."

Chapter Four

"I'm sorry, Stella, but the committee runs things around here and the members have decided that Suzannah stays. She hasn't broken any rules. She's never late for her shift and she's good for business. The customers love how friendly she is with them—"

"And even friendlier with the boss. Except you're not the boss, are you? Not really. You can't fire her. You can't even issue her with a warning. The only thing you can do is make sure you're never alone with her. Will you at least do that? Will you make sure your shifts don't overlap?"

"Of course I will. I've already drawn up a new rota. She'll be on with Mike or Eva when she's not on her own." He hesitated, slouching into the settee.

"What is it? There's something else, isn't there? Something you've not told me." She stood in front of him, hands on her hips.

He looked tired, drained, and pale. This wasn't how it was supposed to be. They had come here to get away from the rush and pressure of the city.

"They're having a séance." "Who is?"

He looked at her, and she knew.

"Oh, no. Tell me you're joking. They can't be having a séance here. Not in the club. I told you what Rhiannon said." Another thought struck her. "Oh God, today's the twenty-ninth of October. Please don't tell me they want to do it on Halloween!"

He said nothing.

She sank onto the settee next to him, head in her hands. "Look, it's been quiet here for a few days. That bolt has stayed locked upstairs, and there haven't been any more bangs and crashes, but if they perform a séance here, they could unleash God knows what. You know what happened to Sarah and Bill Asher. You've got to make them stop."

He stood and went to the dining table. "There's nothing I can do. It's their decision. I'm only an employee here and, as for all that nonsense Rhiannon's been spouting, I've heard everything you said and kept quiet." His voice rose. "I humored you, because I know what you've been through. But this has got to stop. And now's as good a time as any. A bunch of members want to play with an Ouija board. Big deal! It's not as if there isn't a rational explanation for every single thing that has gone on here." He slammed his fist down on the dining table, upending an empty silver vase.

Stella jumped.

Paul's face was twisted with anger. "Damn it, I've had enough of these ridiculous ideas about demons and God alone knows what. People are going to start thinking you're as mad as Pattie. I'm only thankful you haven't been spouting this nonsense downstairs."

Flinching, Stella stared at him in disbelief. She had never seen him like this. What was happening to them? Thoughts of Sarah and Bill Asher sped into her mind as she tried to keep her voice calm and steady. "Paul, we have to leave here. We must."

He glared at her. "That's crazy. Carry on like this and you'll need a psychiatrist."

Rage, a dark shadow, crossed her mind, swelling inside her. She clenched her fists. "For God's sake, Paul, there's something wrong with this place. Suzannah is not who she appears to be, and the very name of this street has dark and sinister connections. Yet, you're quite happy to let the members play with an Ouija board when they haven't the faintest idea what they're doing."

Paul continued to glare at her. All her energy drained away and despair overwhelmed her. She knew that whatever she said he would go ahead anyway. Did it matter anymore? Head in her hands, she was overwhelmed by weariness and defeat. "Oh, very well, have your bloody séance, but I'm having no part of it. I don't understand what's happening to us, Paul. I love you, but I'm beginning to wonder if I even know you anymore. I don't know how much more of this I can take. Maybe I should leave." She started to cry.

Paul was next to her in an instant, drawing her to him. She wanted to push him away, but couldn't. Her tears flowed freely while she was so angry with herself for her weakness.

"Oh, Stella. Please don't go. I'm so sorry about what happened with Suzannah. You know I love you. I always have."

She wouldn't allow him to dry her tears, preferring to accept a clean tissue from him and do the job herself. Finally, she blew her nose and sat upright.

At least he had the grace to look shamefaced. "Look, I know you don't trust Suzannah," he said, "but I'm in a really difficult position here. The facts are there for all to see. She has good ideas that bring in business. Like this séance."

Stella leapt to her feet, brushing away a stray tear. "*What?*"

"You wouldn't believe the number of tickets we've sold. The place is going to be packed." He paused, eying her. "What's the matter now?"

"It was Suzannah's idea? The séance?"

"Yes, didn't I mention it?"

"You bloody well know you didn't!" She couldn't bear to be in the same room as him and rushed out, down the stairs, out of the door, and into the street.

People she knew from the club greeted her, but she stalked past without acknowledging them. She had to get to Rhiannon's cottage. She needed help and protection, and she needed it now.

As soon as Rhiannon opened her door, Stella's terror must have been obvious, for Rhiannon immediately seated Stella in an overstuffed armchair in the comfortably cluttered living room. Slumping, she soon became aware of a cup of chamomile tea being put into her hand.

"It'll calm your spirit," Rhiannon said.

Stella fought to control her hysteria. After a few minutes she recovered herself sufficiently to tell Rhiannon what Paul had said.

As she listened, Rhiannon played with the ankh around her neck. She stood, went to a small antique bureau, and opened a drawer. When she turned around, the Celtic knot pendant dangled from her fingers. "You must wear it at all times to protect you from evil spirits. The next time you see Suzannah, make sure she sees it too and tell me her reaction. Remember, you mustn't take it off, not when you bathe, not at night when you go to sleep, or at any other time. If you are not in direct physical contact with it, it cannot protect you." Rhiannon murmured an incantation before slipping it over Stella's head.

She fingered it, rubbing the bumpy knotwork. "Is that what happened to Sarah Asher? She wasn't wearing it when—"

"When she conceived the child? No. I don't think she was. She must have taken it off, and it ended up in the cupboard. Don't make her mistakes." She paused. "Look, can't you get out of there? Come and stay with me for a while. Come tonight. Make sure you're not there on Halloween."

"I can't do that. I love Paul and I can't abandon him."

"And he won't leave there for you?"

Stella shook her head. "He thinks I'm delusional. He says I spend too much time with you, and you're filling my head with bizarre ideas."

"If only." Rhiannon clasped her hands into the prayer position.

"Please could you come and stay with me on Halloween? I'm not going to the séance, but I could do with some company."

Rhiannon winced. "I'm so sorry, but Samhain's one of our most important festivals. I have to be with the coven."

Stella's spirits drooped. "Of course, I'm sorry, I forgot. It was bound to be important, wasn't it?" She managed a smile and tapped her forehead. "Not thinking."

"Look, it's not ideal, but if you have to stay there, at least you have the pendant. But beware, these spirits can be ruthless and deceitful. They will certainly try and trick you into taking it off if they want you to. Be on your guard."

Fingering the silver pendant, Stella drifted back to the club and went into the busy main bar, where Suzannah was laughing with the men as usual. Paul was nowhere to be seen, but Eva, a middle-aged lady, was also working. At least Paul had kept his word not to work with Suzannah. For now.

Upstairs, he was dozing in front of the TV. He stirred as she entered.

"Want a drink?" she asked, trying to keep it light.

"No thanks." He yawned. "I think I'll go up to bed. I'm really tired."

"It's only half-past nine." But Stella also felt drained from the tension-filled day. She glanced at the cupboard as she went to have a bath. Its door was locked and bolted.

Maybe she had imagined the loosened bolt the other day. Perhaps all the other stuff was the product of some particularly vivid nightmares. And maybe Paul was right and she was spending too much time with Rhiannon. She undressed and removed her watch and engagement ring, placing them on the cistern. In an automatic gesture, she reached for the pendant's clasp, then let her hands drop. She left it on.

Again, she woke at around 2 a.m. to find no sign of Paul. He had been asleep when she came to bed. Assuming he had gone to the bathroom, she turned over. Held her breath as she heard female laughter. Again.

She popped into full wakefulness, threw back the duvet, and swung her legs out of bed. Without switching on the light, she crept along the landing.

More laughter, and she was sure it came from the spare bedroom. She reached the door, which was closed as usual, and listened. Nothing. Slowly she turned the handle and pushed the door open.

There seemed to be two shapes, locked in an embrace. "Oh my God!" She snapped on the light.

Paul groaned and raised his head, looking sleep-befuddled. He was alone in the bed.

"What are you doing in here?" Her gaze raked the room, taking in the bookcase, crammed with hardbacks and paperbacks, the single wardrobe, and small dressing table. No one else was there.

"I woke up and couldn't get back to sleep. I was tossing and turning and didn't want to disturb you, so I came in here."

Stella stared at him. He sounded plausible enough, and he had done that before, months ago when she was recovering from her operation.

"I'm awake now, so you can come back to bed."

Paul turned over and lay back down. "I'm here. 'Night Stella. See you in the morning."

She stood for a few minutes, watching him. What a distance had opened up between them! Wearily, she switched off the light, let the door close behind her, and went back to bed.

Her marriage was in crisis but, for the life of her, she hadn't a clue how to save it.

"You won't be joining us tonight, Stella?" Suzannah asked.

Stella was returning from the supermarket, unloading bulging carrier bags from the trunk. "Not my sort of thing." She tried to keep the edge out of her voice and failed.

"Each to their own."

"Yes indeed." Stella turned to face Suzannah, and sunlight struck the pendant. Was she imagining it or had the girl flinched?

Whether Suzannah did or not, she soon recovered herself. "I'm looking forward to it. I've got the Ouija board here." She tapped a bag under her arm. "Should be a good night. And we're raising money for charity, so it's all in a good cause. Paul will be there, of course."

"No, he won't."

"Yes, he will. Everyone will be working, apart from Mike, who's had to go to Chester. We're expecting a big crowd. So Paul *will* be there." She smirked.

This was too much. "Keep away from my husband, Suzannah."

The girl's dark, kohl-rimmed eyes opened wide. "I don't know what you mean by that, Stella. I have no designs on your husband. What you saw the other day was a bit of fun. A joke." She pointed to her breasts with her free hand. "I get these puppies out for anyone. I'm not ashamed of them. And you're only young once."

Stella felt a million years old. "You don't flash them at my husband. Do you understand?"

Suzannah laughed and walked away, shaking her head.

What a nasty piece of work, Stella thought, watching Suzannah go.

Once darkness started to fall, Stella began to feel agitated. Fingering the pendant, she paced up and down the living room.

Paul was in the bar. They had barely spoken to each other all day but she knew he, as well as she, would be glad when this day was over.

She checked her watch. 6:30. A buffet was being served and she could hear, from the noise, that a lot of members were milling about. Surely with all those people around, nothing really wicked could happen?

She made herself some cheese on toast. Paul was eating downstairs, and the thought of preparing a proper meal just for herself was too much for her tonight. She eventually abandoned half her snack anyway and, finding nothing interesting on television, settled herself down with a DVD of *Casablanca* and a large glass of Chianti.

By eleven, the downstairs had become quiet. Still the odd burst of laughter, but she guessed they were into the séance. As she mounted the stairs on her way to bed, she shivered at the thought of it. And what part was Suzannah playing in the proceedings?

Glancing at the locked cupboard, Stella decided on a shower, then brushed her teeth before settling into bed with the latest John Grisham. Ten minutes later, eyes heavy, she switched out the light.

Paul was merely going through the motions. Pasting on a smile that went no farther than the corners of his mouth, he served beers and shared jokes in the crowded club while Suzannah set up the table for the séance, and Eva worked the back bar until 11:30. After she left, he'd be alone with Suzannah and a crowd of tipsy partiers. His belly twisted at the prospect.

Five members would participate in the séance while the others watched, and Suzannah had volunteered to lead the proceedings. She certainly looked as if she knew what she was doing as she arranged the board with the letters and numbers before placing a small, heart-shaped piece of flat wood in the center. She caught his eye and smiled in that seductive way he wished she wouldn't.

All he could think of was Stella, alone upstairs. As they slipped away from each other, he ached in body, mind, and soul. He had loved her for so long, but recently, they seemed to be moving in opposite directions. Her obsession with that bloody cupboard didn't help, nor did her new friendship with that hippie witch. At the thought of Rhiannon Davies, anger swelled inside him. Everything would be all right if he could get Stella away from the so-called witch.

A voice brought him back to the present. "I gave you a ten pound note, Paul. You've only given me change for five."

"Oh, I'm sorry, Les. Not thinking." Paul opened the till and counted out correct change.

"No harm done. Your good lady not coming to this shindig?"

"No, not tonight. She's feeling a bit tired, so she's having an early night."

"Probably not a bad idea with all the spooks and ghosties that'll be flying around this evening." He laughed. "When are we kicking off?"

Paul glanced over at the clock. 10:45. "Anytime now, I would think." He rang the closing bell. "Ladies and gentlemen, if I can have your attention please." He waited as the chatter died down. A few nervous giggles emanated from various parts of the assembled throng. "Suzannah will be in charge because, out of all of us, she actually seems to know something about this stuff…and it's her Ouija board. She'll need five volunteers." Ten hands shot up. "OK. Les, George, and Roy were first, then Myra and Angie. You can always swap around a bit later. While the séance is going on, I won't be serving drinks because it will disturb the proceedings, so if anyone needs a refill, please get one now."

A few minutes later, with everyone served, Paul switched off most of the lights to a general chorus of "Woooo."

Suzannah sat and directed the other five to do likewise. "I need perfect quiet. As you can see, the letters of the alphabet are arranged around the board with numbers in the middle. In addition to that, the board has the words 'yes,' 'no,' and 'goodbye.' At my direction, everyone is to place their right forefinger lightly on the planchette." She tapped the heart-shaped piece of wood. "You are not to use any pressure. Maybe nothing will happen. Maybe something will. But we must be sure that whatever does happen comes from the world of spirit."

"And not an excess of spirits." Les and the others laughed.

"Please be quiet," Suzannah said. "And those of you around this table, place your right forefingers lightly on the planchette."

Silence descended around the dimly lit bar. "Is there anyone there?" Suzannah called. "Anyone who wants to talk to us tonight?" All eyes were on the planchette. It stood stationary.

At the sound of loud rapping, a collective gasp went up.

"Thank you," Suzannah said calmly. "Can you tell us your name, please?"

"Oh my God, the table's moving!" Myra shrieked, and her hands flew to her mouth.

"It's bloody Les! I can feel his leg moving next to mine!" George pushed his chair back and stood.

"Well, it's only a bit of fun isn't it?" Les said to general jeers.

"I think someone else should take his place," Suzannah said with barely controlled anger in her voice. "If you're not going to take this seriously, we can stop right now."

"No, let's carry on," George said. "Les, you're fired. Duncan, come and join us. You had your hand up, didn't you?"

"Aye, I'll come and join you. And I won't lift the table up either." Duncan Foster sat with the chastened Les behind him, beer in hand.

Silence descended, and Paul watched them through the gloom. Suzannah called out again. "Is there anybody there?"

Nothing.

"Is there anyone at all who wants to speak to us tonight? Anyone?"

The planchette began to move.

"It's spelling out something," Myra said. "Has anyone got a pen and paper to write it down?"

"I have." A voice chirped from behind her. Myra called out the letters "H, E, L, L. Oh God, it's spelled out Hell!"

"O," Angie said with exasperation. "It said 'hello.'"

"Oh that's a relief," Myra said. "It's started again. W, H, A, T, D, O, Y, O, U, W, A, N, T."

"Tell it we want to know who it is," one of the members called out.

"What is your name?" Suzannah asked.

Again, the planchette moved steadily to letter after letter until it had spelled out, "Bill."

"Bill Asher?" Myra asked.

The planchette moved immediately to "yes." Before they could ask anything else, it started moving faster and faster around the board until it finally came to rest.

"What have we got there, Jane?" Myra asked the woman behind her who had been scribbling furiously.

"It says, 'you must stop this before it is too late. He is coming. Go now.'"

Murmurings started, and Paul was tempted to switch the lights back on.

He caught sight of Suzannah's face. She stared straight at him. Paul realized he was coming out from behind the bar and walking toward her, pushing his way through the members who stepped aside to let him pass.

He didn't want to, but was powerless to stop.

When he stood in front of her, her shining, mesmerizing eyes held him captive. The hubbub from the bar faded. *What is she doing to me? What does she want from me?*

"I want you, Paul. You will be mine."

This is ridiculous. Paul shook his head, breaking the trance.

The members' chatter returned. "Are we carrying on?" George asked. "It's beginning to get interesting."

Suzannah turned back to the table, and Paul scooted away, leaning against the bar. He didn't want to even glance at Suzannah again. *I'm going to have to do something about her.*

She looked back at him. *My God, it's as if she can read my mind.* Sick to his stomach, he swallowed hard. He had to leave. Go up to Stella. Try to make amends. But even as he went toward the door, something yanked him back. He couldn't break away. Not yet.

This was all so unreal. Way out of his experience.

All eyes returned to the planchette. The six seated around the table put their forefingers on it and waited.

"Bill Asher," Suzannah called. "Are you still there?"

Nothing.

"Is there anyone else there? Anyone else who wants to talk to us?"

After a lengthy pause, Suzannah shot up from the table.

Everyone gasped, and some giggled nervously.

Paul stared at her. She grew taller, twisted in an unnatural way. She rose into the air. Or did she? From his angle, he couldn't see her feet through the gloom and mass of bodies.

She floated toward him, and he dodged, shoving George aside. Paul apologized absently, intent on putting at least one body between himself and Suzannah. All around her, people drew away to let her through in utter silence, but why? Were they also entranced?

She stopped by the bar and appeared to glide up and onto it before standing and straightening to her full height. All eyes were fixed upon her, Paul's included.

Her feet were bare, exposing oddly long toes, toes that did not touch the bar. She was hovering a fraction of an inch above it. Her feet didn't seem to be taking any weight at all. She was panting, her bright eyes focused on a spot on the far wall.

A spot directly under their apartment.

She opened her mouth, and the voice that boomed forth wasn't hers. It was loud, raw and masculine, speaking some obscure foreign tongue or maybe even gibberish—Paul wasn't sure which.

Everyone remained silent, which was, again, odd.

Why isn't anyone scared, or laughing or something? Anything?

But everyone continued to stare, transfixed, at Suzannah. Finally, she spoke in English, but still in that awful, chilling croak.

"I am Zebullas and I am come again to this place. I will have what is mine. None shall stand in my path. Hear my words and fear them. Hear my words and tremble." She stared down at Paul, fixing him in place.

He was losing his grip on reality. With a supreme effort of will, he tore his gaze away, pushing his customers aside until he could get behind the bar. He snapped on the switches, and light flooded the club.

The reaction was instant. People rubbed their eyes. Some shook their heads. General murmuring started and rose to normal conversational levels. Amid laughter, two men helped Suzannah off the bar.

"I don't know how you did that, but it was great. Really convincing. You should be on the stage," Les said. "Couldn't understand a word you said, but it sounded very authentic."

Suzannah threw back her head and laughed. "Maybe we'll have another go later. The witching hour approaches." She gave Paul another hard stare.

His unease had reached crisis point. "No, that's enough for one night." He was firm.

The members were insistent. Very well, let them have some more, but he wasn't going to stick around for it. He would help Eva clear up the back bar. All the action was in the main bar anyway, so he would leave that for Suzannah to deal with when they finally packed it in for the night. She'd have to lock up. Stella wouldn't approve of that, but the alternative was far worse. He had promised her he wouldn't be on his own with the barmaid, and he wasn't going to break his word if he could help it.

Especially given how Suzannah had unnerved him during the séance.

He glanced up at the clock. 11:45. He checked the back bar, finding it empty. His belly twisted. Of course, Eva had told him she had to leave by 11:30.

Gritting his teeth, he entered to collect used glasses and tidy up.

When he turned, Suzannah was directly behind him, out of sight of the main bar. He shut his eyes to block out the gaze that seemed to tear right into him and lay bare his soul.

She was closer. He could smell her perfume. Expensive. Familiar. The same one his mother used to wear.

"Open your eyes, Paul."

No matter how great his effort of will, hers was stronger.

His lids lifted.

Her eyes were blacker than ever, the pupils and irises enlarged, drowning out the whites. As he stared, he saw shapes reflected in them.

Naked bodies, writhing in ecstasy. With a sudden snap of horror, he realized he was looking at himself and Suzannah.

"No!" he cried and tore his gaze away. He dropped a tray of dirty glasses. They broke, tinkling and smashing. Ignoring them, he raced out to the corridor leading to the apartment. Gasping, he shoved his key in the lock with shaking fingers.

The key slipped from his quivery hold and fell soundlessly to the carpet. He reached and his sleeve slid up, revealing his watch.

12:50.

That wasn't possible. It had been 11:45 a few minutes ago!

What had happened to the last hour? Whatever was going on wasn't natural. And for the first time in his life, Paul Irwin feared for his sanity.

Chapter Five

Stella woke with a start and glanced over at the clock. 12:15 a.m. She was alone in bed, and the apartment was silent. Feeling a sudden urge to use the toilet, she got out of bed without switching on the bedside lamp. She flicked the landing light switch on and went to the bathroom.

By the time she was finished, Stella was fully awake and certain she'd be unable to go back to sleep. She turned on the hall light and went downstairs.

Her heartbeat sped, and she admonished herself.

She was being stupid. Paul was right. They were a bunch of amateurs playing with an Ouija board.

But the apprehension stayed with her. And where was Paul?

She checked the living room. No Paul. The bar downstairs seemed quiet too. She was tempted to get dressed and go see what was up, but in the end, she settled for making a cup of tea and switching on the TV. Flicking through the channels, she came across an old episode of *The Avengers* and immersed herself in the tongue-in-cheek adventures of Steed and Emma Peel for half an hour until she heard the downstairs door open.

She switched off the TV and took her empty mug into the kitchen as Paul came in. He looked surprised to see her.

"Did you have a good time?" she asked as nonchalantly as she could manage.

"Yes, it was a bit of fun." He wasn't short with her but he seemed to be withholding something.

She didn't like that. "Anything happen?"

He shook his head. "There was a bit of knocking and the table moved, until we found out it was old Les having a laugh. Once he stopped, it was all pretty quiet."

"Well, that's good." She didn't believe him.

She knew her husband, and he was keeping something from her.

She didn't like the strange dance of deception they were performing, as though for some reason, neither could say what he or she really wanted to.

He pointed to the pendant around her neck. "Where did you get that?"

Her hand flew up to it. "Rhiannon gave it to me."

"Isn't that the one we found in the cupboard?"

"Yes. It belonged to her mother, but she gave it to Sarah Asher."

"Can I see it?"

After a moment of hesitation, Stella undid the chain and handed it to Paul, who started to examine it.

An enormous crash sounded from upstairs, so loud that the entire building seemed to boom. Stella screamed.

"What the hell was that?" Paul dropped the pendant onto the kitchen counter and raced up the stairs, Stella following.

He checked the bedrooms. "It's the bookcase in the spare room."

Stella joined him and gasped. The bookcase had toppled over and was resting against the dressing table, which had broken its fall. Books were strewn all over.

"But how the hell did that happen?" she demanded.

He shook his head. "No idea. Look, let's leave it tonight, get some sleep, and I'll tackle it tomorrow. I don't want you lifting anything heavy like that."

"Sleep? Who could sleep after this?" Stella looked around. "Is the floor uneven where the bookcase was standing? Could that have been it? Or maybe we overloaded it with too many hardbacks. Perhaps I need to reorganize—"

Paul took her arm. "Look, you won't accomplish anything without a good night's sleep. Let's go to bed, and we'll sort it all out in the morning. It's after one o'clock, for heaven's sake!"

"OK," she said reluctantly. "Are you coming?"

"I'll have a shower and I'll be there." He gave her a light peck on the cheek.

That was the first real sign of affection he had shown her in days.

With the lamp switched off, the room was in darkness. She was drifting off to sleep and in a half- slumbering state of total relaxation when Paul came to bed, snuggling up behind her. Something slid between her legs—his fingers?—and she wanted to wake up properly, but her eyes were so heavy she couldn't open them. He penetrated her, thrusting hard, but making no sound. Still, she couldn't move. He shuddered and withdrew, the abruptness causing a sharp, sudden pain. Her back was stinging, although she had no idea why. She still couldn't open her eyes and was convinced she was dreaming.

She felt him get out of bed and then dropped back into sleep.

When she awakened in the morning, she was alone.

The hot water from the shower stung her back.

Once out, she twisted to look in the bathroom mirror and saw long scratches, scratches that had clearly drawn blood, raking her back. Hands shaking, she picked up her discarded nightgown. The back was shredded and stained with dried blood.

Yet all she could remember was a stinging sensation. Nothing that would have caused all this.

Still holding the tattered gown, she sat on the toilet seat, trying to grasp what had gone on last night.

It had seemed like a dream.

But dreams don't scratch you. Dreams don't draw blood.

In all their years together, Paul had never hurt her. But a lot of things that had never happened before were taking place.

She had to find him and talk it all out. She would have to tell him she wouldn't stay in Priory Saint Michael any longer. No matter what, she wanted out of here. Now.

She touched her throat. The pendant. It wasn't there. She remembered handing it to Paul to look at, but then the bookcase had crashed down. She'd forgotten about wearing the pendant… And where was it?

He must still have it, or maybe it was in the kitchen. She dressed quickly and went downstairs.

Paul was at his laptop in the living room. "Sorry I didn't come up last night. I started watching a film down here and fell asleep on the settee. I woke up at seven and thought I'd get our accounts done."

Stella stared at him in disbelief. "What are you talking about? You said you were going to have a shower and, as I was falling asleep, you came to bed and we… Well, that is, you… Look at these!" Turning, she lifted her T-shirt and showed him the scratches.

"Bloody hell. How did you do that?"

"*I* didn't. *You* did. Last night when you decided to make love when I was too tired to join in."

"Stella, it wasn't me. I'd never do anything like that. I told you. I slept down here last night. I never actually got to bed. I was wide awake after my shower so I came down here and had a brandy. I suppose I was a bit shaken up after the bookcase fell. There was some crappy film on TV, and I fell asleep. I didn't touch you. I swear it."

"Oh, this is ridiculous! So who did it?"

"I haven't a clue." His face contorted, and his voice raised. "Clearly someone made those marks on your back. All I know is, it wasn't me."

He didn't believe her.

He thought she was having an affair with someone and trying to cover it up because of those scratches, which he would have noticed sooner or later.

She burst into tears. "My God, Paul, what's happening to us?"

He closed his laptop and went upstairs. Through her sobbing, she heard him manhandling the bookcase and, when she had recovered herself sufficiently to go up and join him, he was putting the last of the books back on the shelves.

"I want us to leave this place. I want to leave Priory Saint Michael. Today if possible. I want to leave and never look back."

Paul didn't even turn to look at her. He kept putting books back on the shelves. "That's not possible, and you know it. We can't afford it. We have nowhere to go, and I have to give a month's notice anyway."

"To hell with the month's notice! We're not even going to last another week. Paul, *please*."

His face was flushed with anger, and she flinched.

"I trusted you with all my heart and soul and this is how you repay me. Now I know the real reason you didn't want to come down to the séance. With me out of the way, you had an ideal opportunity to meet up with your lover. Who is it? Someone from the club? Or one of those witches you're so busy consorting with?"

This can't be happening. "Paul, there's no one. I swear it. It was *you* last night. Maybe you were sleepwalking, I don't know. But you got into bed with me and you made love but I couldn't open my eyes. It was as if…" A sudden thought hit her. A thought so horrible and bizarre, she could barely take it in. "I have to go and see Rhiannon but if I'm right, we *must* get out of here. Our lives are in danger."

"For God's sake, stop it!"

A part of her wanted to stay and make him believe her, but that would be pointless. Stella saw the pendant on the counter and grabbed it, clasping it around her neck as she raced downstairs and switched off the alarm. Once out of the back door, she didn't bother to reset it.

She jogged down the hill and along the lane to Rhiannon's cottage, praying she'd be in. Stella was in luck. When she showed Rhiannon the scratches and told her what had happened, she could see Rhiannon's expression growing more and more concerned.

"You left the pendant in the kitchen all night?"

Stella hung her head. "I know it was stupid. It's just that Paul asked to see it, and then the bookcase fell over. God knows why—"

"I told you they were cunning. It was a ruse to get you off guard. You were unprotected last night and I am almost certain you were visited by an incubus. He has planted his seed in you. I am as certain of that as I am that the nights you thought you heard a woman's laugh in the spare bedroom, Paul was visited by a succubus. He probably isn't even aware of it himself."

Stella stared in horror. "So what does that mean?"

"The cycle is complete. The succubus has collected seed from Paul. She has mated with the incubus. He in turn has mated with you."

"Much good may it do him because I've had a full hysterectomy."

Rhiannon looked surprised but said nothing for a minute. "He'll know that by now," she said at last. "He'll know you're no good to him. Stella, this is bad. Really bad. You can't go back there."

"But I'm wearing the pendant now. Surely that will protect me. Besides, I have to go back. Will you come with me? Will you explain to Paul what you've told me? Please, I need your help. You're the only one who can do this."

"You don't know what you're dealing with here. It's too dangerous."

"Rhiannon, please. You're my only hope."

Rhiannon started to shake her head, then stopped, as though a new thought struck her. "Very well, I'll come, but we must go to the priory first. I'll ring the vicar and ask to see the old records. I need to be absolutely clear what we're dealing with."

The Reverend Ralph Lewis was a tall, thin man of around sixty-five, with rimless glasses and a quiet air. His calmness and the matter-of-fact way he dealt with their request for information soothed Stella, who managed to draw a deep breath for the first time that day.

He sat at a paper-strewn desk and opened a weighty, old, leather-bound tome. "There are a number of these in the priory archives," he said, with a soft South Wales lilt, "but I think this one will give you the general idea of what they felt they were dealing with in the eighteenth century. The rector at that time was a man by the name of Gwyn Llewellyn and he seems to have been kept pretty busy in the town, especially in Cambian Street." He glanced at Stella. "The street has had a number of spellings, including the present day second 'a' and an earlier form with an 'o' as the last vowel, fitting in with the widely held belief that the street was named after a manifestation of evil known as a cambion. I'll read you an extract from Gwyn Llewellyn's records at that time."

He opened the book at a bookmark. "This is dated during May 1787. 'Was called to the dwelling of Griffydd ap-Gwilym at number seventeen Cambian Street, to find his wife, Hannah, taken to bed of a child who was born in the early morning to much suffering of the mother. The child was without breath and apparently without life and was taken away despite my insistence on its baptism. Also present were Mistress Mallender and Mistress Kendall of Towfleet who sat one on either side of the sadly afflicted woman as she keened and was sorely troubled of a great pain in her belly. Both ladies told of a vision of the devil they had witnessed as the child was being born. They had called out to the demon and asked its name, to be told it was Zebullas and that it had commanded its incubus and succubus to do its bidding.'"

Reverend Lewis looked up. "The entry rambles a bit here and I have often thought that it takes on a slightly hysterical air, as if the rector couldn't really believe what he had seen and heard. I'll pick it up a couple of pages on. By now, the sick woman has died and her husband has been brought in from the alehouse next door where he has been shouting and yelling about devils." He bent his head to the book again, finding his place. "'And I was sore tried to see Griffydd in such a frame of mind as to be mad. At first I thought it to be grief, but then I found him to be possessed of a spirit so evil it threatened to enter the bodies of all who witnessed it. And I took up the Holy Book and thrust it out to him and he fell to his knees with much foaming of the mouth and rolling of the eyes. And he spake in tongues for fully an hour until he was quiet. Meanwhile I prayed for the Lord to cast out the demon. I asked its name and it said it was Zebullas.'"

The vicar took off his glasses and closed the book.

Stella was trying to take it all in. "So, was he successful? Did he get rid of the demon?"

"It appears so, although that name, Zebullas, appears again and again over the years. I first saw mention of it in a diary kept by one of the monks here in the fifteenth century. I'm afraid I can't show it to you as it's housed in the museum in Towfleet. The latest mention I have occurs in 1979 and involves one Sarah Asher."

Stella's eyes opened wide. "Number seventeen Cambian Street wouldn't have been part of the site now occupied by the Priory Social Club, would it?" she asked.

He nodded. "Most certainly. I believe some renumbering occurred in the latter half of the nineteenth century. The club comprises what was number seventeen, the alehouse, and at least one other dwelling-house. Sad to say that all three establishments feature heavily in records of demons and exorcism, especially involving the demon called Zebullas and his cohort of incubi and succubi."

"And what do the books say about Sarah Asher and Zebullas?" Rhiannon asked.

"From memory, I believe it is recorded that she called out that name as she lay dying. She said she could see him in the corner of her room and that he was waiting for her. The vicar was called to the hospital to try to calm her and also to pray with her. He said she writhed on the bed and even at one point appeared to levitate a few inches, but he wasn't sure if that was only his imagination. It was a very frightening, emotionally charged experience and the poor man left the ministry soon afterward."

"So would there be any way of contacting him now?" Stella asked.

"No, he moved to Yorkshire and died following a car crash about ten years ago. My curate used to keep in touch with him."

"Reverend Lewis, do you believe in all this?" Stella asked.

The vicar sighed, leaned back in his chair, steepled his fingers, and gazed upward. "I have been a parish priest for thirty years and I have seen many things I can't explain. Do I believe that evil can take a tangible form and manifest itself? My answer would have to be a resounding yes."

Stella took a deep breath and hoped she wasn't about to offend Rhiannon. "If I needed to call on you to perform an exorcism to cleanse our home of the evil spirits that may live there, would you do it?"

Rhiannon's expression held no anger or resentment, and Stella was relieved. She had been brought up in a nominally Christian home and in desperate times such as this, felt drawn to the old and familiar.

The vicar hesitated before nodding. "I sincerely hope you don't feel the need to call on me for such a service. But I will do it if you require it of me."

"Thank you."

As they left, Stella turned to Rhiannon. "I hope you understand."

"No problem, but you can hedge your bets. I'll give you some oil of protection you can burn in the flat, if you still insist upon going back there. I really wish you wouldn't."

"Let's see what happens when we get there. I've been out for over three hours, so maybe Paul has had chance to rethink and realize there's no way I would do what he has accused me of."

"Stella, I really think that being suspected of infidelity is the least of your problems if you have angered the demon Zebullas."

"Why? Do you know anything else about it?"

"I recognized the name and I think it's because my mother spoke of it. Not surprising I suppose, given her friendship with Sarah Asher and what we've learned."

"Come on, I'll buy you a sandwich in the café and then we'll go and face my demons."

"Don't make light of it, Stella, it's far too serious."

"Believe me, I'm not. I'm trying to deal with it in my own way. I'm facing a crisis in my marriage and for the life of me I can't understand any of it."

Stella glared at the woman behind the bar and drew on the scraps of her dwindling self-control to keep her voice down. "What are you doing here? It's not your shift. Where's Paul?"

Suzannah appeared totally unfazed. She even smiled. "He's not here. He's gone to the Cash and Carry. Mike called in sick, so here I am. To the rescue." Dark eyes narrowed, she scrutinized Rhiannon.

Suzannah shifted her gaze back to Stella. Chilled, she fingered the pendant around her neck. At last, she got a reaction as Suzannah looked away, flinching.

"We'll have a drink," Rhiannon said. "I'll have a glass of red wine. Stella?"

"Large gin and tonic, please." Stella signed Rhiannon in as a guest.

They sat at a table as far from the bar as possible. She had no inclination to sit and watch her adversary flirting with the customers.

They were quickly joined by George Price. "You missed some fun and games in here last night!"

"Oh? Paul said it was very quiet except for Les table-tapping."

George looked a little uncertain for a second, but clearly couldn't resist being the bearer of a bit of juicy gossip. "No, there was plenty going on. Don't know how she did it, but Suzannah started to speak in all sorts of different languages. Well, I presume they were languages. It certainly was neither English nor Welsh and—this is the really good part—she stood and seemed to float over to the bar. Then her voice went all deep and gruff and she yelled out, 'I am Zebedee,' or some such name."

"Zebullas?" Rhiannon asked.

"Aye, that's right. Zebullas. 'I am Zebullas,' she said. Then, just as quick, she was Suzannah as we all know her. It really got to your husband though. He was all white and shaking. I didn't see him for an hour. I went to the gents', heard a crash—I think he dropped some glasses—and saw him dashing off towards your flat."

"What time was that?" Stella asked.

"Oh, around quarter to one. We packed it in soon after."

"So Suzannah locked up?"

"Must have done. She was the only one left on the bar. Anyway, must dash. Promised to pick my wife up after her reading group." He left.

"What do you make of that?" Stella asked.

"Could be a number of possibilities. We can assume that she was left here on her own, so there's no one to say when she actually did leave. She could easily have got into the flat because the alarm wouldn't have been set. All she needed was a spare set of keys, easy enough to get her hands on. While you were talking to Paul downstairs, she could have snuck upstairs, knocked the bookcase over to distract you enough to forget the pendant and hidden in the cupboard until you went to bed."

"She must have some strength to knock that bookcase over."

"If she is what I think she is, she would certainly have strength enough to do that, and much more. You're not dealing with a human." She glanced over at the bar. "Ah, Paul's back."

Stella watched, unseen by her husband, as Suzannah leaned over the deserted bar and kissed him on the lips. Rhiannon coughed, and they both turned in their direction. Suzannah's face held triumph, while Paul's expression was blank.

"I didn't see you there," he said.

Hurt and anger flooded Stella. "Clearly not." She looked from one to the other, then back to Paul. "Upstairs. We need to talk." She motioned Rhiannon to join them, although no one could want to be mixed up in the inevitable row that was to follow.

As the two women passed Suzannah, she hissed. Rhiannon wheeled to confront Suzannah, saying, "I know what you are. Don't forget that. Don't ever forget it."

"What will it take to convince you that Stella is innocent of what you're accusing her?" Rhiannon asked.

"Explain the marks on her back," Paul snapped. Stella flinched at his hostile gaze.

"I can't, and neither can she. But something got into bed with her last night. I believe I know what it is. I believe that it has lain dormant in this flat since Bill Asher left in 1979. I think he threw the pendant in that cupboard as a feeble attempt to keep the demon locked up. Of course, that would never have worked. You need much more than that to keep out a demon like Zebullas. All he needed was for the place to be inhabited again. But not only that, your stupid séance last night finally unleashed his full force, and you will all see the effects of that before long, I can assure you. I can feel the evil in this place. I can taste it." Rhiannon's mouth twisted. "An incubus slept with Stella last night, and I believe a succubus has already slept with you. Maybe you'll find you've lost time you cannot explain."

Paul went white and sank into a chair, his head in his hands.

"Something's happened, hasn't it?" Rhiannon asked.

"It was last night." His voice was a whispery croak. "One minute it was 11:45 and the next it was 12:50, but no more than five minutes could have elapsed between the two."

"Where were you?"

"In the back bar, collecting glasses. It was empty, but then Suzannah was there… She looked at me, and I wanted to get away. There's something about her eyes. It's like hypnosis or something. I remember her perfume. My mother used to wear it."

"Chanel Number Five?" Stella said, remembering his late mother's distinctive scent.

Paul nodded.

"Oh my God, it's true. I *did* smell it on you." Tears spilled over her eyes and coursed down her cheeks.

Paul continued, "I managed to get away and came straight up here. But, as I put my key in the door, I saw it was 12:50. Almost an hour had gone by, but I don't remember a thing about it."

"That's almost certainly when it happened."

And more than once too. Pain stabbed Stella's chest, a hurt so deep and terrible she never wanted to experience it again.

"Do you mean Suzannah…raped him? Surely she was in the bar, conducting the séance?" she asked.

Rhiannon shook her head. "No, Suzannah couldn't have done it. At least, if she's a cambion, almost certainly not, because she can't reproduce. She will be acting as a kind of servant to a succubus. That would have taken Paul's seed from him once she had prepared him. That's how her perfume got all over Paul. She would have entranced him and taken him somewhere they wouldn't be disturbed. Maybe the cellar. All it would have taken is a few minutes. Not even enough for anyone to miss her. Then she left the succubus to do its work. She would also have ensured he didn't remember a thing about it afterward. Meanwhile she carried on with the séance, so no one would suspect a thing. The only question is, who is going to carry the devil's spawn?"

"I don't understand any of this," Paul said. The wretchedness in his voice tore at Stella. She wanted to hold and reassure him, but was too afraid he would reject her. So she kept her distance.

Rhiannon took a deep breath and told Paul everything they'd discovered, including the information supplied by Reverend Lewis. When she finished, Paul, who had listened in horrified silence, finally spoke.

"If you had asked me to believe any of this a week ago, I would have said you were mad. I thought *you* were mad. But after yesterday night, I think you've given me the only explanation that makes any real sense."

Stella had to ask, "Why did you kiss Suzannah at the bar earlier?"

He shook his head. "The truth is I don't know. I can't be around her because something else takes me over. I…do things. I react in ways I don't intend. It's like she gets inside my head and controls everything."

"He's right, Stella. It all fits. That's what cambions do. They are evil through and through."

"Was it Suzannah who killed Pattie?" Stella asked.

Rhiannon nodded. "I think so. Pattie was a danger to her and she knew it. Sooner or later she would have realized what Suzannah really was and would have told you or, worse still, the whole club, when she'd had a few too many. Maybe the members would have laughed it off and thought it was just crazy old Pattie, but Suzannah couldn't take the risk. Besides, she knew *you* would have taken it seriously."

"What would happen if we left here?" he asked. "Would this…thing…follow us?"

Rhiannon shook her head. "Highly unlikely. Given this place's history, it would seem that this demon and his servants stay put. Pity the next person who rents this flat. Mind you, since Bill Asher, none of the other stewards have had any inclination to live here. Until you arrived."

He looked around. "It cost the club a lot of money to renovate it, but it should be boarded up permanently. Or maybe knock the whole place down and build a car park."

"Does this mean we're leaving?" Stella asked.

He sat next to her, putting his arm around her. "We'll stay somewhere local while I work out my notice."

"You can stay with me as long as you like," Rhiannon said.

He smiled at her. "Thanks. We appreciate that a lot, and I'm really sorry for doubting you." He glanced at his watch. "I'll have to go down and start my shift but I'll see you later."

Stella made tea for herself and Rhiannon, all the while reflecting on what had happened. For the first time in days, her spirits lifted. The future was uncertain, that was for sure, but at least Paul understood the danger. The two of them could start putting their marriage back together.

After tea, Stella started packing. "If we're going to stay with you tonight, I'd better chuck some clothes in a suitcase. The thing is, I don't really fancy going up there alone. Would you come with me?"

Rhiannon was about to answer when a piercing scream sounded from the club. They raced down the stairs.

Pandemonium ruled the bar. Hands covered with blood, Eva was screaming, surrounded by people trying to calm her down. Myra was trying to clean Eva's hands with a damp cloth.

"What's happened?" Stella demanded.

Myra raised her horrified face. "Eva's daughter Imogen was raped in the cellar."

"*What?*" Stella cried. "Has someone rung for an ambulance?"

"Yes, and the police are on their way too." Paul came through the cellar door, carrying a young girl of about eighteen, barely conscious. Her legs were smeared with blood. Her dress had been ripped to shreds, and bloody claw marks scored her breasts. He deposited her tenderly upon an upholstered settee, her blood mingling with the deep red brocade. He looked haggard, as if he hadn't slept for a week. Of course, it must be the shock of what had happened, Stella reasoned, but he still looked far more exhausted than the man she had seen only a half-hour earlier.

Kneeling beside Imogen, Stella took her hand. "What happened? Who did this to you?"

The girl's lips moved. Stella leaned closer and caught her faint whispers. "Suzannah… I came to get her… There was a horrible creature. Tried to run but... Suzannah held me down while it..." Imogen passed out.

A policewoman and two paramedics arrived, so Stella and Rhiannon backed away. Eva was still crying, and Myra was rinsing the bloody towel. The paramedics eased Imogen onto a stretcher, with a sobbing Eva helped to the ambulance by the policewoman.

"Terrible business this," Joe said. "Shocking." But Stella ignored him. "Where's Suzannah?"

"Haven't seen her for ages," Myra said. "Eva sent Imogen to find her as it was her shift, and she hadn't been seen for half an hour."

"If she comes back, don't let her out of your sight." She turned to Paul and Rhiannon. Lowering her voice, she said, "Imogen told me that Suzannah held her down while some hideous creature raped her."

"The incubus. It has to be. It chose her," Rhiannon said. "Poor kid."

"The police have got to arrest Suzannah," Stella said, wanting to wring the barmaid's neck.

"I don't think we'll see her again. And I don't think the police will ever find her," Rhiannon said. "She'll have gone. She'll reinvent herself and find other demons to serve."

"So we'll never know if she was Sarah's daughter," Stella said.

"No, but I think it is highly likely."

"So where was she all those years when she was growing up?" Stella asked.

Rhiannon shrugged. "In a safe house, looked after by the woman who delivered her that night, I would think. I imagine she lived miles away so no one would ever guess who she was. She bided her time until the signs were right and she could return to serve her real master, as well as the succubus and incubus who first created her through Bill and Sarah Asher."

"They're still here?" Stella asked, appalled.

Rhiannon nodded slowly. "Yes, but it's all a bit odd, isn't it? I mean I am assuming Imogen can give a description of the creature who raped her. She must have got a good look at him. These are usually creatures of the night. They don't show themselves in their true colors in daylight. In fact, there's something not right about all this. It shouldn't have happened like this."

"Too right it shouldn't have happened!" Stella exclaimed.

"No, I mean…it doesn't fit with what we know of these creatures." Rhiannon seemed troubled and lapsed into thought.

She was the only quiet person in the room, jammed with about fifteen people in the bar all talking about one topic. Paul brought some drinks over, and Stella was about to ask Rhiannon to explain more about her fears when Duncan Foster came through from the pool room.

"Someone's been having a laugh in there," he said, grimly. "It's a right bloody mess."

"What's happened?" Paul asked.

"You'd better come and see for yourself."

Stella, Rhiannon, and Paul hurried through to the pool room to see the balls arranged in a neat pattern in the middle of the table. Its felt was ripped.

"It looks like claw marks," Stella said, exchanging glances with Rhiannon.

"And this could be a pentagram," Rhiannon said, tracing the outline with her finger. Each ball had been placed in a five-pointed star.

"That'll cost a bit to repair," Duncan said.

"I'll get on to the company we use and ask them to come out tomorrow if they can."

"Thanks, Paul. Not been the best of days here, has it?"

Paul shook his head. He swayed, as if losing consciousness. Stella grabbed his arm, and he leaned against her. She was certain if she had not been there he would have fallen.

"What's the matter, Paul? Do you feel ill? Can I get you some water?" She glanced at Rhiannon, who was frowning. "Let's sit you down." Stella and Rhiannon guided him to a nearby chair, and he dropped into it.

A few members looked on with mixed expressions. "Shall we call another ambulance?" Duncan asked.

"No, no, I'm sure he'll be fine in a minute," Stella said. "He needs to rest."

"Stella!" Rhiannon sounded apprehensive. "What's that on Paul's arm?"

"What? Where?"

Paul's sleeve had ridden up as he'd sat. Only half-conscious, he seemed unaware of Rhiannon's concern as she pulled up his sleeve to reveal a bloodied scratch. It formed a single continuous swirl with no jagged edges.

Stella looked at it, and at Rhiannon, fear mounting. "This means something, doesn't it?"

Rhiannon stood back. "It means I was wrong. Terribly wrong."

Chapter Six

"This is something only women can do, Paul," Rhiannon said as she, Paul, and Stella sat around her kitchen table three days later.

In Rhiannon's warm and cozy kitchen, with the smell of apple wood from the old-fashioned stove, all talk of demons seemed incongruous. On the hob, an old black kettle steamed away, providing its owner with water for a seemingly endless supply of herbal teas, while on the walls, bunches of lavender and rosemary hung from hooks, their fragrance adding aromas of summer to the chilly November afternoon. In this timeless sanctuary, they should be talking about mulling wine and baking spiced cakes, not trying to decide how to rid themselves of an ancient evil.

Paul broke into Stella's reverie. "I'm working the evening shift there tonight anyway and I'm worried about the two of you going upstairs in that flat alone and summoning up whatever's in there." He poured himself more merlot with trembling hands, hands that hadn't stopped trembling since the attack on Imogen.

"Imogen's rape proves that this demon and his servants are able to manifest themselves wherever they want to within the club," Rhiannon said. "Something—that bloody séance most likely— released Zebullas and my guess is he's channeling himself through Suzannah. Fortunately, I have protection for us, and my friend Art has sent me all I need by way of invocations. I now know what I'm dealing with, but I can't involve you, Paul, I'm sorry."

Stella watched the exchange. Both were stubbornly refusing to budge but, in the end, the decision had to be Rhiannon's. She was the only one of them who had any idea how to rid them—and the club—of whatever was wreaking such fear.

"There's no better news of Imogen, I'm afraid," Stella said. "I called Eva this morning. Imogen's drifting in and out of consciousness. Nothing she manages to say makes sense. The doctors are baffled because, apart from the obvious cuts, scratches and bruises, she's relatively unscathed physically. She was a virgin before it happened, which accounted for a little of the blood. Whoever...whatever...did that to her was certainly brutal and caused more bleeding, but her wounds will heal.

"They did find out she'll never be able to have children though. Apparently there's something wrong with her internal organs. Probably had it since birth."

Rhiannon raised her eyebrows. "So the rape was all for nothing? That really *is* peculiar."

Paul stood and went to the window, fingering the crystals that hung there, shimmering in the weak sunlight of late afternoon. "I feel so helpless in all this."

"Your natural instinct is to want to protect Stella," Rhiannon said. "I understand that, but this time you have to trust me. Of course I'm scared. I'd be a fool not to be. But I know what I'm doing. Go and work your shift this evening as usual and try not to be alone if you can help it. You've been marked. That scratch on your arm..."

Paul traced the curved outline. "I don't know how I did that."

Rhiannon nodded slowly.

Fear twisted Stella's belly. Rhiannon was holding back information about Paul's arm. And what had she meant when she had said she had been wrong?

Despite repeated attempts to get her to explain, Rhiannon had refused, stating only that she was working on it and would put everything right.

Rhiannon took one last gulp of wine and slammed her hands flat down on the table. "Right! Come on, Stella, let's get this over with." She grabbed the large floppy bag she carried everywhere with her and slung it over her shoulder before reaching into it and fishing around for a few seconds. She pulled out a small vial and handed it to Stella. "It's another oil of protection. We'll anoint ourselves with it now, and then again when we begin our work."

Stella took out the stopper. A heady mix of patchouli and lavender filled the air. "Reminds me of an aunt I had. She always used patchouli. I haven't smelled it for years." She dabbed some on her wrists and neck, rubbing it in as Rhiannon was doing.

"It's powerful stuff. So with that and the pendant you're wearing, you should be protected. Just in case though, Art sent me a special spell I shall cast before we start."

Stella kissed Paul, who flinched. She raised a brow, and he said, "I'm not surprised that stuff protects you. It nearly knocks you over!" He wrinkled his nose and waved it away.

Stella laughed. "We'll see you later."

As soon as they started up the hill to the club, Stella's fears returned and redoubled. "I hope your friend the High Priest knows his stuff, because I'm so scared, I can't even think straight." Without Rhiannon, Stella would have turned round and run down that hill as fast as she could to get away from what they were about to do.

The mere thought of going near that cupboard, let alone opening it and summoning whatever resided there, chilled her to the core. But, as Rhiannon had said, the *thing* was no longer confined to the cupboard. It had the run of the club. Customers were staying away. Since Imogen's rape, word had got round that something wasn't right. Some of the older members were starting to talk about the days of Sarah Asher.

Mike was behind the bar, alone. "You're the first two people I've seen today."

"Anything been happening?" Rhiannon asked. "I'll show you. In the pool room."

The two women exchanged worried glances and followed him. The pool table had been repaired but, once again, the balls were rearranged into that distinctive shape.

"They were like that yesterday morning when I got here. A couple of the lads had a game here and put the balls back in the frame. When I went to lock up, there they were in this shape again. Then again this morning. I put them back in the frame, but when I went back an hour later, they were like this. No one has been in here today and we only had six members in all day yesterday. I don't know what's going on, but I'm handing my notice into the committee. I've had enough. The place will be closing down soon anyway because we can't carry on like this. I'll work my week's notice but that's it. Eva's leaving as well, but she's signed off sick anyway so you won't see her here again. Suzannah's gone, so that leaves Paul and a couple of casuals."

"We won't be here much longer either," Stella said.

"They're staying with me at the moment. We've come to get some more of their stuff," Rhiannon said.

"Yes," Stella said. Mike didn't need to know the real reason for their visit. He was so unnerved already, he would quite possibly have walked out, notice or not.

"Paul OK?" Mike asked.

"So-so. He'll be in later for his shift though." "Come on, Stella, let's get going," Rhiannon went to the door. "Oh, I'd leave those balls as they are," she said lightly.

"Well, it doesn't look as if anyone's going to be playing pool today anyway so I might as well."

As they were going upstairs into the apartment, Stella was curious. "Why did you tell Mike to leave those balls as they were?"

"Protection. You're going to be seeing a lot of pentagrams when I get my chalk out."

"But who's been arranging the pool table balls like that? Surely the spirits we're dealing with wouldn't do anything to protect us?"

"Sometimes a good spirit tries to help out. There is a good spirit here. Maybe it's Bill Asher, I'm not sure, but he's very weak. He can't compete with the evil. Oh!" Rhiannon's face contorted, and her eyes started streaming.

"Whatever's the matter?" Stella grabbed Rhiannon's shaking hand.

"I'll be all right in a minute. Can't you taste it? It's foul. And the smell!"

Stella could neither smell nor taste anything apart from the lavender and patchouli.

Screaming surrounded them, the howl and rush of a sirocco wind blasting toward them from upstairs.

Rhiannon seized Stella's arm with one hand. "It's out. It's definitely out. It's right here!" She took a piece of chalk from her coat pocket and scribbled a large pentagram on the kitchen floor tiles. "Quick! Get inside here!"

Stella jumped inside it, clinging to Rhiannon, who said, "Sprinkle your oil of protection. All around you and around the pentagram. Copy me. *Now*!"

The screaming wind was almost on them. Stella dropped to her knees and obeyed, sprinkling her oil, too terrified do anything other than copy Rhiannon and hang onto her at the same time.

Then *it* came. And this time Stella could not only see and hear it, she could smell it.

An ugly, reeking pall of black smoke shot into the kitchen and hovered around the outside of the pentagram, encircling them. The unearthly shriek deepened into a loud roar, like a firestorm.

Rhiannon was chanting in some arcane language. In the center of the smoke, a shape was taking form. Its eyes blazed like red, hot coals. Stella heard screaming and realized it was herself but she couldn't stop. Her flailing hand caught in the pendant and broke the chain. It fell. Something was trying to pull her out of the pentagram, and Rhiannon yelled at her to stay put.

Stella clung tighter and tighter to Rhiannon, who started chanting again. The shape was almost fully formed, but still surrounded by the smoke that swirled, stopping short of the pentagram. It was like nothing Stella had ever seen before. Its hideous, reptilian head was angular, the oval red eyes menacing. It had no apparent ears and a thin, serpentine body which writhed and swirled.

It opened its mouth, and its voice was a hiss. At first she thought it wasn't forming words, but realized it was one word repeated over and over.

"Zebullas."

Still Rhiannon chanted over the noise of the demon, repeating her invocation time and again, her voice never wavering while Stella could feel herself losing consciousness.

"Stella, stay in the pentagram. Don't let any part of you stray over the edge."

Her vision was darkening, her head throbbing.

She lost control and fell to the floor. The last thing she heard was Rhiannon screaming at her to stay in the pentagram.

She awoke to the sun streaming through the window of her bedroom in the apartment. Paul was coming in with a cup of tea. She rubbed her eyes. "What time is it?"

"Morning, sleepyhead." Paul set her cup on the bedside table and bent over, kissing her on the cheek. "Just after nine. You certainly slept well last night."

As she tried to clear her head, memories started to flood back. The kitchen. Rhiannon. The demon. "Oh my God!" She threw back the duvet. "What am I doing here? What are you doing here? We have to get out, Paul. We have to."

Paul hugged her, holding her close. "Shh, Stella. Come on, you've been really poorly and you've had a nightmare, that's all. A really vivid nightmare."

"But the demon. You remember. Imogen's rape. The cambion…Suzannah."

Paul laughed. "I haven't the faintest idea what you're talking about. Who's Imogen? And Suzannah? It's all part of your dream. You had a complete breakdown, you know. You've been pretty much out of it for a couple of weeks. Now get back into bed and enjoy your cup of tea."

"What's today's date?" "November sixth. Why?"

Stella shook her head while her thoughts tumbled around in her mind. The last she remembered, it had been November fourth, sometime in the afternoon, and now it was the morning of November sixth, so she had lost a little over a day. But that was nothing compared to what she was expected to believe.

Had her befuddled brain managed to dream up weeks of horrific supernatural activities? She wasn't a particularly imaginative person, so that was more incredible than the events themselves.

"Paul. Where's Rhiannon?"

"Rhiannon?" He didn't seem able to place her for a moment. "Pattie Davies's sister? The hippie witch? Don't know, at home I should imagine."

"We're supposed to be staying with her."

"What?" He laughed again. "My God, that was some dream!"

"We're supposed to be leaving here. When Imogen was raped in the cellar and—"

Paul sat on the bed and took Stella's hand. "Look, love, I know it must seem real to you, but I haven't faintest idea who you're talking about. No one was raped in the cellar, and I've never heard of anyone called Imogen."

"She's Eva's daughter."

"Eva's daughter is called Amy, and she lives in Canada."

"She must have another daughter."

"OK, that's it, I'm calling the doctor again. He's going to have to do something. Try and rest and I'll call him."

He left her, and she lay back on the pillows, fighting with herself to remember. The last thing she recalled was falling unconscious in the pentagram. She remembered the demon's face, its terrible hissing voice. "Zebullas," it had said.

Could she really have made all this up? Maybe if she could go down to the club. Talk to the people down there. If she could contact Rhiannon. That was it. She needed to speak to Rhiannon. She looked around but couldn't see her bag and, therefore, no cell phone.

Paul came back and squeezed her hand. "He'll be here within the hour. I'm really worried about you, Stell. I know you've been bad but this is something else."

"I need to call Rhiannon. I'll feel better when I've spoken to her."

"I didn't even know you two knew each other."

Stella blinked. "What? Don't you remember Pattie's funeral? There was just Rhiannon, her coven and me."

Paul was visibly resisting the urge to laugh.

"Paul, are you saying I imagined that as well?"

"Not Pattie Davies's death. She was killed by a hit and run driver late at night when she'd had a few too many. As for the rest, it's news to me."

Stella was quiet for a few moments. "So are you telling me that there isn't something evil in our landing cupboard?"

This time he gave in and laughed. "Oh yes, there's an evil mess in there and I must make time to sort it all out. But if you mean do we have an evil spirit lurking in there? Well, let's say he'd be very short of space."

His cell rang, and he took it out of his pocket. "Thanks Mike, yes, I'll come down and let him in." He shut off the phone.

"The doctor's here. He's come in through the bar, so I'll go and get him."

Stella pushed off the duvet and struggled to get up. Her legs weren't obeying her too readily but she managed to haul herself upright.

She needed to go to the bathroom. Taking a deep breath, and steadying herself by leaning on the wall, she edged along the landing. She switched on the light to get rid of the dark corners and stopped when she got to the cupboard. She stared at the bolt. Not the new one Paul had put on, but the old one. *Don't tell me I imagined that as well!*

She heard voices from downstairs. Paul called, "Stella, the doctor's here."

"I'll be there in a minute," she replied and opened the bathroom door.

Minutes later she made her way back down the landing, a little less wobbly on her feet.

In her room, a doctor she did not recognize smiled at her. "I hear we've been having some nightmares since I last saw you."

Stella sat on the edge of the bed. "I don't know what they are, doctor, but I'm pretty sure I've never seen you before in my life."

She saw Paul mouth, *I'm sorry* to the doctor and saw his dismissive gesture. "It's all perfectly normal in your condition, Stella."

"What do you mean 'in my condition'?"

"My dear, you've had a complete mental breakdown," the doctor said. "The stress of what you went through with your operation and the subsequent treatment all took its toll. The added pressures of moving house, changing your entire life. It was too much. The brain has a way of protecting itself in these situations and in your case it said enough is enough and you had a breakdown. I need to prescribe some mild anti-hallucinatory drugs and you'll be fine. They may take a week or two to kick in, and you may feel drowsy, but it's all part of the healing process."

Stella stared at him. "Doctor, are you sure we've met before?"

"A few times."

"Why don't I remember you?"

"As I said, you were out of it. You were rambling a lot. Not nearly as lucid as you are now. You seemed to have a fixation with demons."

"We put that down to one of the last conversations you had before your breakdown," Paul said. "It was the night Pattie Davies came in here and was regaling you with all sorts of nonsense about a previous steward and his wife."

"Sarah and Bill Asher? So at least that part was true?"

"Oh yes, Joe was quite concerned at the effect it had on you. Pattie died that same night, and the next day you collapsed. You've been ill ever since. Today's the first day I've heard you string a coherent sentence together…even if the subject has been a little bizarre." He laughed.

"You didn't change the bolt on the cupboard?"

"What bolt?"

Stella shook her head. "Could I have my phone, please? I want to call Rhiannon."

The doctor handed a hastily scribbled prescription to Paul. "One of these three times a day with water. No alcohol. I'll see you again in a week's time, Stella. At my surgery. I think it's time for you to get up and about again."

"Thank you, Doctor," Stella said, relieved that at least now she would be able to go down to the club, call Rhiannon, and find out how much of this was imagination.

Paul saw the doctor out and brought her handbag. She found her cell phone which had some power left in it. She searched for Rhiannon's number but it wasn't there. "I know I had it."

Paul shook his head, looking concerned. "Honestly, Stell, to the best of my knowledge you've never met her. But I can describe her to you."

"That wouldn't do any good, I'm afraid. I've never met the lady either."

Stella searched her brain for something else. "Is Eva on the bar tonight?"

"Yes, she is, as a matter of fact. She's on from six."

"She shouldn't be. Not if my memories are correct. But clearly they can't be." If Stella was right, Eva was never coming back to the club, so the mere sight of her serving drinks, with a smile on her face, would tell Stella what she needed to know...and what she feared—that her memories of the entire past two, or maybe three weeks, were pure fiction.

"I'll get dressed."

"Don't you think you should wait until you've started taking those pills? Give it another day, love. I'll ask one of the members if they'll go to the pharmacy and I'll stay with you."

Stella hesitated. She did feel weak but wouldn't get any stronger lying in bed. "At least let me get dressed and come down to the living room. I'll read a book or watch TV and this evening, I can go down to the club. I can always have orange juice."

"OK, but that will be enough for today. No venturing outside or trying to track down hapless witches."

"Promise." She managed a weak smile, and Paul kissed the tip of her nose.

She entered the kitchen with some trepidation, but all was normal. No chalk marks on the floor, no trace of oil. But that could have been cleaned. She went through into the living room, followed by Paul.

"Fancy some toast?" he asked.

"That would be nice, thanks," she replied.

Everything was all so normal, so homely and, as she ate the toast and golden honey Paul prepared for her, she looked over their DVD collection. Morning TV was the usual rubbish, all shopping programs, chat shows, and ancient reruns of garbage that hadn't been particularly watchable the first time around. Her eyes settled on *Blithe Spirit* but she decided Paul wouldn't approve in the circumstances, so she selected *Airplane* instead. She wanted a good laugh. Paul joined her and pretty soon she was lost in the comedy, laughing until her sides ached and starting to feel better than she had in weeks…whatever the truth of those weeks might actually have been.

The rest of the day passed pleasantly. Looking out of her window, she could see the rain and wind buffeting the leafless trees, and people huddled in coats battling their way up and down the hill. Stella was glad not to be out there. At least here, she felt safe and could start to put her own demons aside.

Later, showered, with makeup on and hair washed, she dressed in jeans and a black sweater, then went downstairs into the bar.

She got a warm welcome.

"It's good to see you, Stella. And you look much better than last time I saw you." This was from Joe. She almost asked him when that had been but decided that would sound too weird.

Eva stood smiling behind the bar, handing change to one of the members. Goosebumps pricked Stella's skin. Acknowledging Joe's good wishes, Stella made straight for the bar.

"Hello, Stella. How lovely to see you." Eva started to reach for the bottle of gin.

"I'm on orange juice at the moment. Alcohol doesn't mix with the pills. How are you, Eva?"

"Me? Oh the same as always. A few aches and pains, but I can't complain." She poured juice into a cut crystal tumbler.

"Have you heard from your daughter recently?"

"Amy? Yes, she was on the phone only last night. They're coming over for Christmas so it will be lovely to see my grandchildren again. Haven't seen them for two years."

"Did I hear that you've got another daughter?"

Eva's face drooped. "No, not anymore, dear. Died at birth. Buried in the priory churchyard."

"Oh, I'm so sorry. I must have heard wrong."

"No harm done. It's a good many years ago."

Stella took her juice and sat at one of the tables. Suddenly she remembered something. The pendant. Her hand flew to her throat though she already knew it wasn't there.

Seeing Eva Sharpe laughing with customers rather than hysterical over her daughter's rape was the proof Stella needed. Her nightmares had been so real and so vivid but that's all they'd been: nightmares. The cambion, incubus, succubus, and the demon Zebullas were all figments of her imagination. Stella inhaled deeply, looked around the room and wondered when the purple drapes had been hung.

Chapter Seven

Over the next month, she set about rebuilding her life. She began to help in the bar, came off the anti- hallucinatory drugs, and started walking around town, venturing down to the Cash and Carry for supplies and going into nearby Towfleet to get her hair done and buy a new dress for Christmas.

She and Paul were stronger than ever, although that first evening had brought a shock, when Paul had taken off his shirt to reveal a scratch exactly like the one she had imagined in her nightmare.

"Caught it on a nail in the cellar. Hurt like hell at the time and it ripped my shirt. You must have seen it when I got ready for bed one night and it fed into those nightmares you were having. Anyway, good job my tetanus injections were up to date. God knows how old that nail was. Needless to say it is not there anymore."

One morning, with the frost crackling underfoot, Stella decided to have a proper tour of the ancient priory that had given its name to the town.

Generations of families who frequented the club were buried in its peaceful churchyard. This was a small community, and people seemed reluctant to leave it, except for Eva Sharpe's Amy, who had met and married a Canadian.

The old church was beautiful inside as well as out, and Stella was alone as she walked around, examining the wall plaques recording past lives and familiar surnames. She saw names such as Lloyd, Price,

Hughes, Jones, and Llewellyn. The stained glass window depicted lives of the saints, with the largest scene devoted to Saint Michael, killing demons.

Stella sat for a few minutes, enjoying the peace and stillness, before embarking on a wander around the churchyard. Here, more souls lay peacefully under their gravestones marked by the same familiar names. She located Sarah and Bill Asher, but no grave for the stillborn baby. Around the corner, she caught sight of the name 'Sharpe,' perhaps a relation of Eva's.

Stella went closer to find the gravestone partially obscured by a lower branch of an overhanging tree. She pushed it out of the way to read, "Imogen Sharpe, born first March 1981, lived only a few hours. Much beloved daughter of Eva and Frederick."

Stella dropped the branch and stepped back, nearly tripping over another small gravestone. How could she have imagined that? How could she have thought up that name?

She had to talk to Paul about it. She hurried out of the graveyard, nearly slipping on the frosty ground.

The air was bitterly cold, and her breath formed a cloud in front of her.

While climbing the hill, she caught sight of someone on the opposite side of the road. A woman with long coppery hair, dressed hippie-style in a long red coat, with a massive floppy bag over her shoulder.

"Rhiannon!"

The woman stopped, turned, and looked straight at Stella without a shred of recognition.

"Rhiannon, please. I have to talk to you. It's Stella. Don't you remember me?"

Stella started to cross the street. Too late, she saw a car heading toward her. It screeched to a halt, and that was the last she knew.

"She was very lucky not to have been killed. That driver had good brakes, but if he hadn't reacted so quickly, she wouldn't be here today. You can take her home with you later, but if she reports anything strange, like seeing flashing lights or any kind of visual disturbance, you must bring her straight back."

"Thank you, doctor." Stella recognized Paul's voice through the fog in her throbbing head as she struggled to open her eyes.

A bright light shone above her. It, along with the familiar smell of antiseptic, told her she was in a hospital bed.

"Thank God. Can you hear me, Stella?" Paul asked.

She tried to speak but her mouth was too dry. "You were in an accident, but you're going to be all right. We think you slipped on a patch of black ice when you were crossing the road." He held a mug of water with a straw to her lips.

She sipped, and this time when she opened her mouth, she managed to utter a few words. "Rhiannon was there. I called to her."

"I know." Paul smiled. "She looked after you until the ambulance came. She's here now. We've come to take you home. Do you want to see her?"

"Please."

A familiar face framed by shiny, raven-black hair came into view and gazed down at her with those dark eyes.

Stella screamed.

"Stella. *Stella!*"

She opened her eyes to see Rhiannon peering down at her. They were both sitting on the kitchen floor.

"Thank goodness. I thought I'd lost you when that thing dragged you out of the pentagram."

"What's going on? Where am I?"

"You're in your kitchen. Don't you remember? We've been trying to get rid of that demon, Zebullas."

"But that was weeks ago, before my accident. No, that's not right. It never happened. I don't know you. Oh God!" Stella put her head in her hands and wept. "I don't know what's true anymore, Rhiannon. I think I must be out of my mind. The last thing I remember is Suzannah looking down at me. I was in hospital after a car accident, and Paul said she was you. Oh, none of this makes sense."

Rhiannon helped her to her feet. "Come on, I'll pour you a brandy."

They sat in the living room while Stella tried desperately to clear her head.

"So you're saying that the last two months that I remember never happened? That it's still November fourth?"

"That's right. You fainted as you were being dragged out of the pentagram and I suppose that's when the demon placed the hallucinations in your mind. That was a couple of hours ago, and I've been trying to get you back ever since." She sighed. "I'm afraid I have some terrible news for you."

"What is it?" Stella couldn't imagine there could be anything as bad as what she had been experiencing.

"I saw the demon's face." She wrung her hands. "I'm sorry, but Paul and Zebullas are one and the same."

"*What*?" Stella shot to her feet, staggering slightly as a wave of lightheadedness hit her. "No, you're wrong. It can't be. I've been married to him for fifteen years. No! I don't believe it."

Rhiannon put her arm around her. "I'm so sorry, but I'm afraid there's no doubt. That mark on his arm. It's a zeta, the sign of Zebullas."

"But someone did that to him. Suzannah maybe."

"No," Rhiannon said quietly. "He did it to himself. And we must go to him."

"What do you mean?"

"We have to cast him out for good, Stella. You're the only one who can do it. I know that now. We have to go to him."

"Where?"

"Come with me."

In a flash Stella knew where Rhiannon would take her. "Not into that cupboard."

"It's the entrance. We have to go in there."

"No, I can't." Stella shook off Rhiannon's arm, but her friend gripped her harder and hauled her out of the living room, through the kitchen to the stairs. In her dazed and troubled state, she couldn't protest anymore. She was too weak and confused by everything that had happened.

"Trust me, Stella, I know what I'm doing. And we are protected."

Stella's free hand went up to her throat. "The pendant. It's broken. It must still be in the kitchen!"

"You don't need that now. We have stronger protection. Come with me. It's going to be all right."

The cupboard door was wide open and, as Rhiannon steered her through, Stella caught sight of the bolt. It was the new one Paul had fitted. Once inside, Rhiannon found a flashlight. He must have left it inside, Stella realized dazedly.

Rhiannon clicked it on and shone it through the doorway. She pushed the Christmas tree aside.

Behind it a narrow staircase led down. A greenish glow emanated from its foot, illuminating the steps.

"I'll go first and hold your hand to steady you."

All Stella wanted to do was run, go down to the club, and find some normalcy in all this confusion and horror, but she told herself that she was in safe hands. Even if she didn't understand what was going on.

At the foot of the short staircase, a corridor opened out onto another room. Purple drapes lined the walls, and, recognizing them, Stella gave a start. "I've seen these drapes before. They were—"

The woman turned. Suzannah.

She laughed. "Did you honestly think Rhiannon would have brought you down here?"

Stella reached for the nearest wall to steady herself, too shocked even to scream or utter one word.

"I have enjoyed playing with your mind, Stella. You have a strong spirit. Rarely do I have such an interesting challenge, but I'm growing tired of our little game. It's time to end it. Come with me."

Suzannah's eyes bored into Stella's, hypnotic, mesmerizing. She was unable to stop following the cambion farther into the room. Against the far wall was an altar draped in black with a ram's head device and a large gold emblem she recognized from Paul's arm. The zeta. The mark of Zebullas.

In front of the altar was a long table and on it, a man lay. Naked.

"Paul!" Stella tried to get to him but couldn't. Something—Suzannah's power?—held her fixed to the spot.

"He can't hear you. He's mine now."

"You lied to me. He's not the demon. *You* are!"

Suzannah's laugh was raucous and grating. "Oh no, Stella. Rhiannon knew. She guessed I was a cambion and she was right. But she was wrong when she said Paul's seed would find no home in me. My Lord Zebullas has given me the power. He mated with the girl Imogen and took her fertility, then planted it in me. I am his as Paul is mine. Soon I shall bear a child. A child of Lord Zebullas. Poor barren Stella. It could have been so different. You could have been spared. If Lord Zebullas had found a womb inside you, he would have planted his seed in you and you would have been blessed."

Stella stared at her, speechless, nausea welling inside her as she realized who…*what*…had entered her that night.

Suzannah picked up a huge gleaming sword, raised it above her head, eying Paul. Stella could see her husband's naked chest trembling with the beating of his heart, the heart that Suzannah would surely cut out.

"No!"

Suzannah smiled, renewing her clenched-fist hold on the sword as footsteps thudded on the wooden floor, coming closer.

Her expression changed. Her face twisted, and her grip faltered as she looked behind Stella at…at…

A strong male, Welsh voice rang out. "In the name of God the Father, Son, and Holy Spirit I command thee to leave."

Stella was released, free to move. She turned to see Rhiannon and Reverend Lewis. The vicar wore his vestments, held a Bible and an aspergillum from which he sprinkled holy water. Rhiannon was chanting, summoning her ancient spirits.

Stella spun back around. Suzannah was hissing, the sword wavering in her hands. On the table, Paul stirred. Stella rushed to him, shoving Suzannah, who fell to the floor, writhing and screaming. Her sword tumbled out of her hands and clattered on the wood.

Paul's eyes opened. "Help me, Stella!"

Hands quivering, she struggled to loosen his bonds while Rhiannon and the Vicar continued the exorcism.

Suzannah roared and clawed for Stella's neck. "He's *mine*!"

"No, you evil bitch, you will *not* have him." Stella dragged Suzannah's fingers off her neck and pushed her away. A brief waft of Chanel Number Five was replaced by the vile stench of carrion.

The cambion lost her balance and fell, only to leap to her feet, baring her teeth. They were jagged.

Rotten. Not the perfect white teeth of Suzannah the barmaid.

Stella tugged at the last of Paul's bonds, breathing through her mouth to avoid the awful reek of the cambion's foul breath.

The room began to vibrate, as the scream of the sirocco rose and came closer.

The vicar stepped forward and shook the aspergillum so that holy water showered down on Paul and Stella. When it hit the cambion, its skin began to sizzle and blacken. It let out another roar.

The demon wind came closer. Paul rolled off the table, and Stella grabbed the altar's black velvet cover, sending chalices and gold plates crashing to the floor. She flung it around him.

"Come on, hurry, we have to get out of here," Rhiannon yelled.

Stella grabbed Paul's hand. He was still dazed and not fully conscious. Together with Rhiannon, they urged Paul to the stairs. The vicar was already at the exit. He pointed behind them, and the other three turned to look at bright flashes of red and yellow amid the shrieking wind.

A brilliant white light flooded the room. A vision appeared, so bright that they had to shield their eyes. It had enormous wings and a gleaming sword, but Stella couldn't make out its features. It was locked in battle with a snakelike something that swirled, hissed, and transformed itself, over and over, into different hideous serpentine forms.

Two other bright figures appeared, joining the fight. Flames shot out into the room from the vision, licking at the drapes, which started to smolder.

"Come on. Let's get out of here before this place goes up like a tinderbox!" Rhiannon shouted over the din. They could hear the fire alarm ringing from inside the club.

"Yes, let's leave the blessed Saint Michael to his work." The vicar started up the steps. They scrambled through the cupboard, ran through the apartment, and back down into the club.

The vicar wrenched open the door. Outside, in the freezing darkness, a small crowd was amassing, drawn by the sound of the alarm and the roaring of the flames that could be heard coming from the club.

"Someone call the fire brigade!" one of them shouted. Others rushed to help Rhiannon and Stella as, between them, they half-carried Paul out of the main entrance. From inside the club came the sound of thunder, and flames shot through the roof.

"Bloody hell. What was that?" "Must be a firebomb."

"Looks like a firework factory went up."

Flames of green, blue, and red—unnatural fire that consumed the building, tearing through it— snarled and crackled as a fire engine could be heard in the distance approaching fast. The flames shot high up in the air with a mighty roar.

"Was there anyone in there?" George asked. "You wouldn't believe it if I told you," Rhiannon said.

"Is it over?" Stella asked. She and Paul huddled together, shivering from cold and fear.

"Yes, I believe so. Saint Michael always prevails," the vicar said serenely.

"With a little help from the Lord and Lady," Rhiannon said, smiling at him.

He said nothing but winked at Stella.

A huge weight had lifted from her heart.

Chapter Eight

Stella looked out of Rhiannon's living room window at a beautiful spring day. The magnolias and cherries were in bloom, and she saw her first butterfly of the year—a red admiral—fluttering from blossom to blossom.

"Fancy going to the pub for a drink?" Rhiannon asked as she rummaged in her bag for a tissue.

"That would be nice. We can see how they're getting on with the new flats while we're at it."

"All I can say is, I wouldn't want to live there, even though it *has* been exorcised."

Stella shook her head. "No chance. Paul and I are very happy with our little flat above the greengrocer's. He's starting work on Monday."

"Yes, it's taken a long time for both of you to recover, but I'm so glad you decided to stay here."

"Despite what happened at the club, it's a really nice little town and the people are lovely. Everyone has been so supportive, even if they don't understand what went on. Sometimes I wake up in the morning and wonder which reality I'm in. Even now." She smiled.

"Yes, but at least now you can laugh about it." Stella shuddered at the memory. "I really thought I'd lost it. I thought I'd gone completely mad. The first two months were unreal. In my mind, I'd already lived them and I had to keep reminding myself that *those* two months were illusions placed in my mind by Suzannah."

"She was certainly a powerful one. I'll never forget how scared I was when you fainted and your leg slipped out of the pentagram. That awful demon smoke was on you in a second and it dragged you into it. I was pulling and pulling at you, but it was too powerful."

Rhiannon's voice was becoming more agitated with the memory of that terrible day. Stella comforted Rhiannon with a hand on her arm. She had told the story countless times already, but Stella guessed it was part of Rhiannon's healing. One day she would come to terms with what she had witnessed. One day, hopefully, they all would.

"When the demon took you and the smoke disappeared back upstairs, I knew I couldn't do any more alone. That's when I went to get the vicar. Fortunately the club was empty when we got back even though the door was unlocked."

"It was Paul's shift, remember. Suzannah had taken him by then."

Rhiannon nodded. "Anyway, it didn't take a genius to work out where Zebullas had taken you. The rest you know, but Reverend Lewis said he'd never experienced anything like it, even though he has performed loads of exorcisms over the years. Remember, you're not to spread that around. He likes to keep those activities quiet. I'm so thankful I knew about him, but that was only because a friend of mine had seen him do it once. He was pretty impressive then as well."

"He must be well thought of in high places if he can summon up the chief angel to do his work."

"Zebullas was a major demon. A major demon needs a major angel. And I like to think the Lord and Lady helped as well."

"Isn't it a bit unusual to mix pagan and Christian like that?"

Rhiannon shrugged her shoulders. "Maybe it is. But I've always been one to keep an open mind and believe there is power and truth in all the spiritual beliefs. If our faiths show they exist, as they did then, and can join together to defeat a terrible demon, who are we to say that only one way is right and all the others are wrong?"

"True. But you told me that, despite all that happened, Zebullas isn't dead."

Rhiannon shook her head. "Demons can't die but they can be banished back to Hell. And that's what will have happened."

Goose pimples rose on Stella's arm and she hugged herself. "Paul says he can't remember anything from the time he arrived at the club for his shift. I've never really understood why you didn't want him involved."

"Because I knew Zebullas—or rather Suzannah—wanted him, and I couldn't protect you both. As it happens, I couldn't even protect you. Not at first anyway."

"By your actions, you saved Paul's life and you almost certainly saved mine as well."

Rhiannon waved her arm in a dismissive gesture. "Come on, let's go and get that drink we promised ourselves."

They walked along the lane and turned into the High Street, making their way up the hill toward where the club had stood on the corner of Cambian Street. Now it was a building site.

"Foundations are in," Rhiannon said.

"Yes, I suppose they'll be built by the end of the summer, judging by the way things are thrown up these days."

"As I said, nothing could tempt me to live there."

"Me neither. I wonder if they'll tell the purchasers what went on here."

"Not that anyone really knows, except us."

"True. Even the firefighters were at a loss to explain how the blaze started and how it burned at such a high temperature so fast. Although the gas tanks they used for the beer would have helped."

"They didn't find any bodies though. That's the one thing that puzzled me," Rhiannon said. "I would have thought they would have found Suzannah. But it's this cambion thing. The vicar and I have concluded that she must have changed herself into demon form and gone with Zebullas."

"Come on, I'm thirsty." Stella turned away from the building site and they continued their walk.

Across the road, a large black dog watched them climb up the hill before returning her gaze to the construction. After a while, she lumbered off, her stomach distended. Soon she would give birth and needed a comfortable, safe place for herself and her pup.

Suzannah was back.

About the Author

Following a varied career in sales, advertising and career guidance, Catherine Cavendish is now the full-time author of a number of paranormal, ghostly and Gothic horror novels and novellas.

Her novels include: *Those Who Dwell in Mordenhyrst Hall, The After-Death of Caroline Rand, Nemesis of the Gods, Dark Observation, In Darkness, Shadows Breathe, The Garden of Bewitchment. The Haunting of Henderson Close, The Devil's Serenade, The Pendle Curse* and *Saving Grace Devine.*

The Crow Witch and Other Conjurings is a collection of her previously published and brand new short stories.

Her novellas include: *The Darkest Veil, Linden Manor, Cold Revenge, Miss Abigail's Room, The Demons of Cambian Street, Dark Avenging Angel, The Devil Inside Her,* and *The Second Wife*

She lives by the sea in Southport, England with her long-suffering husband, and a black cat called Serafina who has never forgotten that her species used to be worshipped in ancient Egypt. She sees no reason why that practice should not continue.

You can connect with Cat here:

Website: catherinecavendish.com/
Facebook: facebook.com/CatherineCavendishWriter
X (formerly Twitter): twitter.com/Cat_Cavendish
Instagram: instagram.com/catcavendish/
Tik Tok: catcavendish
Bluesky @catcavendish.bsky.social

Curious about other Crossroad Press books? Stop by our website:
http://crossroadpress.com
We offer quality writing
in digital, audio, and print formats.

Subscribe to our newsletter on the website homepage and receive a free eBook.

www.ingramcontent.com/pod-product-compliance
Lightning Source LLC
LaVergne TN
LVHW050935080826
845145LV00004B/1265

* 9 7 8 1 6 3 7 8 9 0 2 3 3 *